THE WITCHES' REVENGE

A PONYTEER STORY
Book Two

BY

T. F. CARROLL

PEN PRESS PUBLISHERS LTD

First published in Great Britain by
Pen Press Publishers Ltd
25 Eastern Place
Brighton
BN2 1GJ

ISBN13: 978-1-906206-26-0

Printed and bound in the UK

A catalogue record of this book is available from
the British Library

Cover design and
Illustration by Alexa Garside

To my dear grandchildren
and children everywhere
who enjoy reading a story

ACKNOWLEDGEMENT

Thanks to my wife, Joyce, for her constant enthusiasm and patient editing. I think Joyce is truly magical.

ABOUT THE AUTHOR

T F Carroll

Thomas Carroll was born in Yorkshire in 1923. He flew in Lancasters during World War II and then retrained as an air traffic controller. After serving for twenty years in the RAF he worked for twenty years in the oil industry. He settled in Cheshire after retirement to be near his grandchildren and his first stories were told to them as bed-time stories until one day they said, "Granddad, why don't you write them down?" – he has been writing ever since!

Also by T F Carroll are books one and three in the Ponyteer trilogy, *The Angry Witch* and *Witches on the Run.*

CHAPTER ONE

SHOCKING NEWS FOR THE PONYTEERS

"Hi you guys, come and see this."

A couple of hikers heading for the Sandstone Trail turned their heads to see if the girl with the American accent was calling to them. They saw her sitting on a golden coloured pony and looking at a notice nailed to a tree that stood at the entrance to the Tea Pot Café. Three other girls also on ponies joined her.

One of the hikers said to the other, "She wasn't talking to us."

"I know, but I was just thinking, you don't hear many American accents around these parts, do you? She's probably here on holiday. People come here for a bit of peace and quiet, you know."

"She'll get plenty of that. Nothing ever happens in Tinsall."

But they were wrong. Both of them were wrong. They were wrong about everything.

Laura, for that was the name of the girl with the American accent, wasn't in Tinsall on holiday. She lived there. She had been living in Tinsall with her grandparents ever since her father and mother had been killed when a robot called Jupiter had exploded in San Francisco over three years ago. Her parents' friend, Professor Klopstock, had been badly injured in the same accident and Juno, another robot caught in the explosion, had been severely damaged before she had mysteriously disappeared.

As for "Nothing ever happens in Tinsall," how could you expect those hikers to believe that in this small Cheshire village, Laura and her new English friends, known to the locals as the Ponyteers, had been involved in adventures with robots, discovered Roman Treasure and been threatened by witches and aliens.

The hikers were just starting out on the Sandstone Trail and unknown to them they would soon reach that part of Tinsall Hill where most of those adventures had taken place.

"What is it, Laura? What is it?" one of the girls called out.

Holding the reins in one hand, Laura used her free hand to point to the notice. The other three girls inched their ponies into position so they could read it. Lindsey, on her pony, Poppy, was to the rear of Leanne and Alison, so she had to stand in her stirrups to read the notice over their shoulders.

The notice read:

TEA POT CAFÉ
Under new ownership

NOW OPEN
Props. Fred and Bessie Nightingale

Morning coffee – Lunches – Afternoon teas
Homemade scones and cakes our speciality

"So, they're the new owners. I'm surprised anyone would want to buy it. You know – considering what happened. But that notice sure does bring back the memories," said Laura.

"You can say that again," exclaimed Alison. "And they're all bad. That Mrs Potts, it gives me the creeps just to think about her."

Her friends nodded and there were some muttered words of sympathy.

To be fair, Alison had just cause to feel bad about Mrs Potts, the previous owner of the café. After all, it was only a few months ago that Alison, Professor Klopstock and Lindsey had been threatened at gunpoint by her and locked in the café cellar. Alison shuddered when she recalled how a swarm of dwarf, alien, warlike creatures had forced them along an underground passage that led from the cellar to a cavern under the "dark side" of Tinsall Hill and there they had been thrown into captivity.

Lindsey shivered too. But it wasn't because of her shared memories with Alison. She shivered because she felt cold. She looked up at the sky, it had been a fine warm morning when they had set out, but now clouds were beginning to hide the sun. She remembered her grandma saying, "You can expect anything from the weather at Easter time. Grandma was right of course. Yesterday, for instance, they'd had hail, sleet, snow and thunder!

"I think we should make tracks for home," Lindsey said. We've got to think of the ponies."

A biting wind had sprung up; the Ponyteers hunched their shoulders against it and headed for home. They knew that Lindsey was right.

Laura was leading the way. She stopped when they were halfway down the hill. Pointing and speaking almost with

3

awe in her voice, she said, "Gee you guys, take a look at that." She was pointing to the fertile Cheshire plain that stretched out below them. Herds of fat cattle were grazing on lush green fields of grass interspersed by fields of rich brown earth that were already showing signs of early spring crops. Still speaking with awe in her voice, Laura said, "There's not a trace of snow on the plain, but see the Welsh mountains beyond, they're covered in snow."

"Thank your lucky stars we've got those mountains," said Alison. "If they hadn't been there all that snow would have been dumped on us!"

"Oh, gee – right," said Laura.

Leanne looked up, her face to the wind, and said, "Wind's from the north. If snow's on its way, those mountains are on the wrong side of the plain to stop it getting to us."

"Well, even you can't do anything about that, can you, Leanne?" Lindsey said with a mischievous grin on her face.

Leanne took a friendly swipe at her sister. Then, giving her pony, Peace, a gentle tap with her heels, she led the way down the hill. "Come on," she called. "If it snows it'll be worse up here on the hill. Don't let's take any chances."

They got into line quickly and followed her.

After making sure that their ponies had been fed and warmly stabled the girls went to see Leanne and Lindsey's grandparents, who lived almost next door to the riding stables.

Leanne was about to knock on the door when it flew open and out hurtled her young brother, Alex, hotly pursued by his friend, Ginger Tomkins. They almost knocked Lindsey and Laura flying…

"Alex, what do you think you are playing at?" Lindsey yelled, angrily.

"Sorry Lindsey. Sorry Laura. Sorry everybody. Can't stop. Kick off's in 15 minutes and I've forgotten my shin pads," cried Alex, and the two boys ran off without a backwards glance.

The girls were still standing at the door talking angrily about Alex and Ginger and boys' bad behaviour in general when Grandma appeared and invited them to come into her warm kitchen and have a cup of tea. Granddad, who was reading the local paper, laid it on the table as soon as he saw them. His face was flushed. He didn't even say "hello" he was too excited by what he had read in the paper. He stabbed a finger at the print. "What do you think about that?" he said.

"What's it say, Granddad?" asked Lindsey.

"Those Eastlys," Granddad stuttered. "The ones who stole your ponies. Says here they're letting them out early. Getting out early for good behaviour." He snorted. "Good behaviour, I ask you!"

Alison spluttered over her cup of tea and her hands trembled as she dabbed a tissue to her lips.

Speaking as calmly as she could, Leanne said, "Fancy that, Granddad, getting out early? I can't believe it."

The others looked at one another without saying a word. How could any of them tell Leanne and Lindsey's grandparents that Mrs Eastly was a witch? How could they tell them that they had been in the witch's den at Red House Farm? And how, without causing them to be worried and anxious, could they explain that the witch blamed them because she was locked up in prison and had threatened vengeance against them? They couldn't bring themselves to do it, so as soon as they could they thanked Leanne and Lindsey's grandparents for the tea and said it was time to go home.

The instant Leanne lifted the latch, the door was flung open and they were met by an icy blast of wind that carried a flurry of snow into the kitchen.

"It's started then," said Granddad. "I could feel it in my bones. Quick girls, before we get snowed under." And for a brief second or two he stayed at the door and watched as the girls turned up their collars, bent their heads low against the wind and started up the road. Closing the door behind them, he added another log of wood to the fire before settling down in his favourite chair to read some more about Mrs Eastly.

They'd taken only a few strides when Laura noticed that Alison's face looked terribly pale. She said, "What's the matter, Alison, aren't you feeling well?"

"Scared more like. I'm frightened that when that witch gets out of prison she'll come and get me." Alison was looking up at the sky and all around, as though she was expecting, at any moment, to be scooped up and carried away.

"Well, she can't get you tonight, Alison. Mrs Eastly is still in prison – remember? We'll go with you, make sure you get home – okay?" It was Leanne who had responded to Alison's fears, and linking arms with her friend, she laughed and said, "Hold on tightly, Alison. What with her weight and the two of us, her broomstick would never get off the ground!"

"Thanks, Leanne." Alison managed a weak smile and squeezing the comforting arm that held her, she said, "I wish I were brave like you, Leanne, but I'm not. Old witch face, she'll try to put a spell on us. I know she will." Her voice sounded weak and anxious.

"Just let her try it on, that's all," said Leanne. "She'll be in for the surprise of her life when she comes up against Juno. Huh! She doesn't know we've got one of the cleverest robots in the world to look after us, does she?"

6

"Surprise of her life? She'll get the *fright* of her life," said Lindsey, adding weight to her sister's words. "Don't forget, Juno's read all the spell books that were in the witch's den. So, if Mrs Eastly does try it on, she's the one who could finish up being a spider or a toad." Lindsey paused, then added, "Ooh! If only she would – try it on, I mean." And the gleeful look on her face was proof that she really would like old witch face to try to cast a spell on them.

"Yeah," said Laura. "You're right, Lindsey. If she does try it on, she could end up being a toad. Well, she could. Wow! And the size of her, she'd be the fattest toad in the world!" The thought of it made Laura splutter. The splutter turned into a laugh. And she laughed and laughed as though she would never stop.

Laura's laugh was infectious, so too was her humour, and they all wanted to share and add to it. "What about changing her into a beetle, or a mouse, or a rat?" They were all at it now, competing one with another to see who would come up with the funniest, or most horrible thing, to turn the witch into. It was fun while it lasted. And while it lasted, their fears about the witch were forgotten.

"You okay now, Alison?" asked Laura, when the laughing had ceased.

"Thanks – yes. But the sooner we tell Juno about the Eastlys, the better. I'd feel a lot safer then," said Alison as they reached her garden gate.

"We can't tell her 'til tomorrow," Laura called out. "Today, she's at Jodrell Bank, remember?"

"Oh right, I'd forgotten." Alison paused as she opened the gate. "I could make it to Juno's workshop tomorrow about eleven. Does that suit? Juno will tell us what to do then, won't she?"

They all agreed that an eleven o'clock meeting was fine. Alison left them and went up the garden path. She stopped at the door to give them a final wave and rang the bell. The door opened and she went in.

They were leaving Alison's house when Laura suddenly remembered she had something to tell them. "Oh, I'm sorry Lindsey. Ever so sorry Leanne – I almost forgot. The professor phoned. All that news about Mrs Eastly's early release, that's what made me forget. Listen. And boy, will this cheer you up." Laura was almost dancing on the pavement she was so excited. "It's Jupiter," she said. "He's the first robot to fly solo into outer space and he's made it! Hear that, you guys? He's made it! And you know something? The 'gentle people' he helped us rescue from those dwarf warlike aliens under the hill – well, they're home! Jupiter's landed them on Petranova. They're all safe and sound."

It took a second or two for the news to sink in, then, Leanne called out, "Three cheers for Jupiter." And without caring who heard them, they all joined hands and gave Jupiter three rousing cheers.

When the noise from the cheering had died down, Laura spoke again. She said, "That's not all I've got to tell you. There's something else." She held up her hand, "Now, guys, hear this for good news. It's Jupiter and he's on his way back. The professor says Juno's in touch with the scientists at Jodrell Bank and, any day now, we'll know exactly when he'll be back with us in Tinsall."

Good news? It was great news! And for the second time, within minutes, there was silence while the news sank in.

"Wow! Good news? It's the understatement of the year, Laura. Don't you wish the professor could be with us? Can you imagine the look on his face now the dream of his life has come true?" Leanne was as excited as Laura and so were the others. And the cheering began all over again.

"Wish I could go to Petranova," said Lindsey, wistfully, after the cheering had died down. "But Mum and Dad, I don't think they'd let me go."

"Well, it's not as if you just wanted to go to Blackpool is it?" Laura said, digging Lindsey playfully in the ribs, then adding seriously, "But if the opportunity does come along, perhaps they will let you go, Lindsey. You never know with parents, do you?"

Leanne didn't say a word. She didn't share her sister's newfound interest in space travel. Lindsey knew that and so she dropped the subject.

Laura felt it was time to go home. She said goodbye to her friends and started on her way. Once she was alone, thoughts about Mrs Eastly, the witch, crowded into her mind and she, too, like Alison, began to feel afraid. It was getting dark early and shadows took on strange and terrifying shapes that seemed to be following her. She kept looking over her shoulder to see if they'd gone away. They hadn't, they were crowding in on her and seemed closer than ever. No matter how fast she walked, they were still there. She started to run and only when she was inside the cottage with Granddad and Grandma did she feel safe again.

Leanne and Lindsey arrived at the door of their house at the same time as Alex; he explained that the match had been abandoned at half time because of the weather. He rubbed his hands together to try and get some warmth into them. "I'm looking forward to having a nice hot bath," he said with relish.

"In that case," said Lindsey, "I'll ask Dad to put out the flags."

"What do you mean?" said Alex. A look of suspicion had spread over his face.

"Well, usually it takes the whole family to persuade you to have a bath, doesn't it? This is the first time I've heard you volunteer. That's what I mean," said Lindsey.

Alex stuck his thumb on the end of his nose and wiggled his fingers at her. He was first through the door when it opened.

By this time the snow was coming down in large wet flakes and Leanne and Lindsey were glad to get into the warmth of the house.

Lindsey went to bed early, she felt tired – it had been that sort of day. She lay in her bed with her eyes closed but she could see her Granddad as plain as plain as if it were day. She could see him reading out the news to them about Mrs Eastly's early release and how angry it made him. The news didn't make Lindsey angry; it made her frightened – more frightened, perhaps, than the others. She had a feeling that the witch had it in for her especially, more than Leanne, Alison or Laura – and she knew the reason why – and when. It had happened on the day they had rescued their stolen ponies from Red House Farm. When Mrs Eastly saw them ride away, she forced her twin stepsons to ride with her in the jeep to pursue and try to capture them. But, before Mrs Eastly could catch and put a spell on them, their ponies had carried the girls to safety, across a wide and muddy stream. Too late did Mrs Eastly see the stream and too late did she scream for the driver to apply the brakes. The jeep teetered briefly on the water's bank, then gently nose-dived in. And as Mrs Eastly and the boys emerged from the stream all muddy and wet, Lindsey had laughed out aloud and called them monsters from the deep! It was the laugh that did it. Lindsey shuddered when she recalled

the baleful look she'd received from Mrs Eastly after she'd laughed.

But odd though it may seem, there was an element of good news mixed in with the bad as far as Lindsey was concerned, and it was this – Bill and Andy, Mrs Eastly's stepsons, were being released from custody at the same time as their stepmother. And why was this good news for Lindsey? It was good news because the day she and Alison had heard the twins play the violin at a school concert Lindsey had fallen for Bill and Alison had fallen for Andy. It was Lindsey and Alison's secret. No one else knew about it, not even Laura or Leanne, and certainly not the twins! But when they were alone together, Alison and Lindsey talked about them all the time.

Before she finally fell asleep, Lindsey was thinking what she would say to Bill if they accidentally met in the street. And she wondered whether he would forgive her for laughing at him and calling him a monster from the deep.

In the meantime Mrs Eastly was languishing in prison where she was paying the price for her misdeeds. Apart from the stolen ponies, the police had found her house full of stolen goods, but did Mrs Eastly blame herself for her plight? She did not. She blamed the Ponyteers! And as each day of her sentence passed, her anger against the girls grew. At night she would lie in her bed and recite the most dreadful spells she could think of, spells she would cast on them once she was free. Oh, the pleasure of it. It helped Mrs Eastly to fall asleep and dream sweet dreams of revenge.

The snow had turned to rain during the night and by morning all the snow had gone. When the girls walked down to Juno's workshop the sun came out and shone in

11

a clear blue sky. There wasn't a single cloud to be seen. It was eleven o'clock and all the girls had turned up on time.

Alison looked up at the clear blue sky, and without thinking, she said, "Great day for flying."

"Not for broomsticks, I hope," said Leanne, with a smile.

"Don't joke about it, Leanne," said Alison, feeling sorry she'd mentioned the word flying.

They arrived at Juno's workshop to find the door wide open. Without knocking or calling out to say who it was, they trooped in.

The robot didn't look round, she knew perfectly well who were coming through the door.

"Co-me in gi-rls, the-re's some-thing I wa-nt you to see," she said, in her usual chopped-up way of speaking.

She was working on some equipment, the major part of which looked like a large television screen. But, before Juno could say any more, the girls blurted out the news about Mrs Eastly's early release from prison. "What are we going to do, Juno? What are we going to do?" they asked, fretfully.

Juno didn't reply. Instead, she pointed to a toolbox lying on a workbench just a few metres away. Slowly the box, unaided, raised itself from the bench and the girls watched with open mouths as it moved through the air and settled itself on the table next to the screen on which Juno had been working. Again the robot gestured. This time the lid of the box opened and a screwdriver flew out of the box and settled neatly into the palm of her hand. She walked across the room to the girls. Her legs squeaked. For a moment it reminded them of the professor, who called her Miss Squeaky Legs, which was funny, because he now had an artificial tin leg that squeaked just as much as hers.

"Now, what's all this nonsense about being afraid of

Mrs Eastly?" Juno asked, her voice sounding more staccato than ever, and the red light in the centre of her forehead blinking merrily. She spoke again and said, "Poor witch, I feel sorry for her. I suspect she can't remember half of her spells and one day she'll probably end up turning herself into something quite horrid!" She placed a metallic hand to her mouth and a sound, not unlike laughter, escaped through her fingers.

Juno's little demonstration of magic had restored the girls' spirits and they now felt secure and happy again. "Oh Juno," they cried, "no wonder the professor said we could rely on you." Juno smiled and gave them a little theatrical bow to show how much she appreciated the trust they placed in her.

She saw them looking at what appeared to be a large television screen on which she had been working. "I know what you're thinking," she said. "But no, its not a television screen, it's a radar visual display unit. Look, let me demonstrate." She pressed a switch; there was a soft purring sound and a finger of light, pivoting in the centre of the tube, turned round in slow circles picking up tiny specks of light in its travels.

Lindsey was first to spot them. "Look, Juno. Those little bright lights, what are they? And they seem to be moving across the screen."

"That's because they are moving," said Juno. "Those little dots of light are either aircraft or birds." She went on to explain that the aerial that turned on the workshop roof sent out signals in all directions, and when the signals struck an object, say an aircraft or a bird, the signals came bouncing back like echoes and were displayed on the tube as little white lights. "You *hear* the echoes that come bouncing back when you yodel or call out aloud in the mountains, but you *see* and not hear the echoes that come bouncing back from radar signals."

Everybody nodded to show that they understood.

Then Leanne came up with the fifty thousand dollar question. "How can we tell which of those little white echoes on the screen are from Mrs Eastly and her broomstick – it could be any one of them?"

"Yes," said Alison, with a tremor in her voice, "How will we know it's not Mrs Eastly on her broomstick, coming to get us?"

"Because, I paid a visit to Red House Farm," said Juno. "Don't you remember?"

"Yeah, but what happened?" said Leanne.

"Sad, really. The very first things I saw when I entered the house were the shattered remains of two violins that were lying on the floor of the kitchen. And it had been no accident – I could tell."

When Lindsey and Alison heard that coming from Juno, they gasped out aloud and nearly divulged their secret feelings for Bill and Andy.

"But," said Juno, "To answer the questions raised by Alison and Leanne, I also paid a visit to the witch's den and made a few minor adjustments to her broomsticks."

She paused and waited for Alison and Leanne's reaction.

The reaction didn't come from either of them – it came from Lindsey. "You mean you bugged them?" she said. Lindsey was very much into spy stories and Juno's claim to have made a few minor adjustments to the witch's broomsticks intrigued her immensely.

"That's right, Lindsey. And now, whenever those broomsticks take to the skies, they will leave a trail so we can tell to whom they belong and where they are going," said Juno. "Wherever and whenever she flies on her broomstick, a tiny letter 'W' will trail across the screen and follow her."

"Brilliant, Juno," they all cried. " 'W' for witch, what a clever idea."

"And those other special looking marks on the screen, what are those," Laura wanted to know.

"Oh, this one's the workshop," said Juno, pointing with a metallic finger. "And that's where you live, Laura," she said, pointing to a different mark on the screen. She moved her finger again. "And this one's where Leanne and Lindsey live. It's so I can keep an eye on you at home. Whenever the letter 'W' appears on the screen a buzzer will sound to alert me and within seconds I'll be told of her probable destination and time of arrival. Poor Mrs Eastly, what a fright she'll get if she tries it on and finds me waiting for her."

"That's just what Leanne said, but just one last question then we'll leave you in peace," said Laura. "What do the locals think about robots living in the village, Juno? Do they treat you okay? I mean – you know."

Jupiter made a sound as if she were a cat purring and the red light in her forehead blinked in a merry fashion. She said, "I know what you mean, Laura. Don't worry. Ever since Jupiter rescued the 'gentle people' from under Tinsall Hill and flew them back to Petranova, we've been treated like local heroes. People pop in at all times of the day to have a little chat. And the butcher next door never misses saying 'Good morning, Miss Juno' when he opens his shop and 'Good night, Miss Juno' when he closes it."

Oh yes, the girls could see that Juno was very happy. And when they said "cheerio," they too were happy and they weren't afraid of Mrs Eastly anymore, because Juno was protecting them.

CHAPTER TWO

RELEASED FROM PRISON

It was her last night in prison and Mrs Eastly couldn't sleep. She prowled up and down in her cell like a cat seeking a fugitive mouse. She was as full of hate as ever, especially for the Ponyteers and more especially for the one who had laughed at her family and called them monsters from the deep! And despite the fact that her house on Red House Farm was found by the police to be stuffed with stolen goods when they raided it, she blamed the Ponyteers for everything. "Just wait 'til I get out," she muttered. "Just wait 'til I get out."

She heard a tap on her cell window, looked up and saw five helmeted heads bobbing up and down outside. She recognised them at once, it was Red Leader with the rest of her aerobatic broomstick chicks. Mrs Eastly groaned. They had been to see her in prison once before to tell her they had been keeping an eye on Red House Farm whilst she was away and had reported signs of robot activity in the grounds. Robot activity? Crazy! Mrs Eastly took no heed of it. She thought Red Leader was a real pain in the neck with her shouts of "Tally ho!" and "Go! Go!"

and "low level" this and "high level" that. She stopped groaning. At least Red Leader was someone to talk to, someone who might help her get through the last lonely night in her cell.

She opened her cell window as far as the retaining stop would allow it to go. "Hi there, Red Leader," she called, with phoney cheerfulness. "What brings you here this time o' night?"

"Your cousin, the commandant, sent us, Sister Bertha," said Red Leader. She was balancing hands free and sitting as casual as could be on her specially built exhibition broomstick.

"Mabel, what does she want?" came Mrs Eastly's curt reply.

"Wants you to know that she will pick you up by car, tomorrow, twelve noon. That's when you are to be released, isn't it?"

"Yes, that's right. But what about the twins?"

"She's arranged for them to be picked up by another driver. You should all be at Red House Farm by three o'clock in the afternoon – latest. That's what she reckons!"

"Oh, does she now?" Mrs Eastly growled. "Anyway, thanks for coming to see me, Red Leader."

"All in a night's work, Sister Bertha. Anything else we can do for you?"

"No thanks," said Mrs Eastly. All she wanted to do now was to get to bed, switch on her brain and try to work out what her cousin Mabel, the commandant, was up to. Why was she picking her up personally and accompanying her to Red House Farm? And why were the twins to be taken to Red House Farm in a different car? Surely they all could have squeezed into that great big car of her cousin's? Mrs Eastly was puzzled.

18

"Right," said Red Leader, "if you don't want anything else, we'll be off then," and she barked out an order, "Red flight, in line astern, low level flight back to base, maximum speed – Go! Go! – Tallyho!" In no time at all Red Leader and her chicks were out of sight.

Mrs Eastly groaned again. As she lay for the last night on her hard prison bed she fretted and tried but still could not find answers to the questions that puzzled her. Finally she drifted off and fell into a troubled asleep

Next day, Bertha was released and escorted back to Red House Farm, arriving at precisely three o'clock in the afternoon. On the way home the commandant didn't say a word. The stern look she had worn on her face during the journey was still there when they went into the house.

The twins had arrived earlier.

The commandant dismissed her driver and asked the twins to take a walk outside so she and their stepmother could talk in private.

Mrs Eastly waited until the door closed behind the twins then she turned to face the commandant and demanded to know what all the privacy stuff was about.

"To save you embarrassment, Bertha," replied the commandant quietly.

"Me? Embarrassed? What the blazes are you talking about? Why should I be embarrassed?" said Mrs Eastly, angrily.

"Bertha, please. It's difficult for me as it is. Please don't make it worse by adopting that attitude. I'm here on official business and what I have to say, you may find embarrassing said in front of the twins. That's what all this privacy stuff, as you call it, is all about." The stern look remained on her face.

Mrs Eastly was getting redder and redder. She said, "I can't believe this. I simply can't believe what I'm hearing.

First it's privacy and now you're going on about official business. Think I'm daft or something? Don't you dare try to fob me off with all that official business guff. If you've got something to say, Mabel, spit it out and get it over with." She glared at her cousin. "You're not talking to one of your young sprogs now you know."

"Very well then," replied the commandant. "I'll give it to you straight. My fellow officers all agree that something has to be done about you even if you are my cousin."

Mrs Eastly sneered. "And what have your fellow officers decided to do to me – shoot me? Go on, tell me," she challenged.

The commandant ignored her. Striving to remain calm she took some papers from her briefcase. "It's a list of charges," she said. "It's a long list, but I will read out just a few of the charges levied against you, Bertha. First, to deal with your admin." She looked at her notes. " 'Lamentably poor', that's what it says here. Take, for example, Amendments to Orders. Hopelessly out of date, and so on and so on. Surely you must realize that neglect in keeping your Amendments up to date makes you a menace – as far as safety is concerned – not only to yourself, but to others around you as well."

Mrs Eastly scowled, but she had no answer to the charge and she lapsed into a surly silence.

Next, the commandant produced Mrs Eastly's flying logbook from her briefcase.

She opened it and placed it on the table for her cousin to see the note that was attached to it. It read simply: "No flying hours recorded for the past two years!" But over that two-year period it listed a number of flying accidents for which the authorities had proven her to be responsible. "What do you have to say about that?" the commandant asked. Mrs Eastly maintained her silence.

"You, you were to blame. I have here the reports from the Courts Martial. And do you know the word that they came up with most frequently?"

Again, there was no reply from Bertha Eastly.

"I'll tell you the word. Incompetence! That's the word. Your incompetence!"

Still no reply from Bertha Eastly, only black looks.

"And finally," said the commandant, "Just a brief word about your spell books. You clearly haven't studied them in years. I'd be surprised if you could remember how to turn a rat into a mouse. Can you?" Mrs Eastly couldn't.

The commandant collected the papers and log book from the table and returned them to her briefcase. "Very well then," she said. "As from tomorrow, someone will run a check on you every day, for a period of at least four weeks. It's for your own good. Try to get you up to scratch. Get you to fly again – safely! Oh, and by the way, a word of warning: forget about seeking revenge on those children in the village. They've done you no harm. Any harm done is of your own making. Do anything to those children, anything at all, and you will be dealt with most severely. I mean it, Bertha. This is an official warning. Do you understand?"

"Yes," Mrs Eastly snapped.

"One last thing, Bertha," said the commandant, fastening her briefcase, "and it's personal. Over the years I've watched you bring up those two boys and what I have seen has hurt me more than you will ever know. Many a time I've shed tears over those poor children. And I'll tell you something else. There are those in the New Order who believe you should still be in prison because of the wicked things you made them do. There now, is that straight enough for you?"

Mrs Eastly couldn't contain herself any longer. She was shifting the weight of her heavy frame from one leg to the other as she spat out the words, "So, that's what they believe, is it? Well now, let me tell you something. You and those busy bodies want to mind your own business. The way I brought up those children has nothing to do with you, or anybody else for that matter."

"Really?" replied the commandant, raising her eyebrows and striving to remain calm. "And what about the boys? Has it nothing to do with them, either? Well, I've got news for you, Bertha. The boys are fed up with the way you brought them up to lie, cheat and steal, and they want no more of it. They are coming up to 18 now and have decided they want to be out of your life forever. Did you hear that, Bertha? They want to be out of your life forever."

"Liar, liar," screamed Mrs Eastly. "Bring them in and let them say that to my face. Go on!"

"All in good time," said the commandant. "But first let me tell you that when they were in youth custody they learned what it was like to be away from your wicked influence. All they now want is the opportunity to live as decent citizens, Bertha. They want to develop their talents further – music, painting and leatherwork. The New Order has made them a grant – bought them an art shop in Chester. The work they did in custody is absolutely fantastic. We put it on exhibition in the art shop a few days before they were released and already their order books are full. Please, Bertha, if you have any decency in you at all, give way to them on this one. Alright?"

Mrs Eastly was wicked, very wicked, but she was no fool. Before her cousin had finished talking she realized that she had lost the battle. "Right then," she said, trying to put on a dignified air. "Let them get on with it. Let them find out what it's like to be on their own and without me to hold their hands."

The commandant asked the twins to come into the room. When they were told that their stepmother had agreed to let them go and lead a new life they were almost overcome with joy. At last they were out of Bertha's clutches. No more humiliation if they didn't steal things for her and no more fear of magic spells. For the first time in their lives they felt they had a future and it looked bright. And for the first time in their lives they were happy – really happy – as they said hasty goodbyes and left Red House Farm and its evil past behind them.

CHAPTER THREE

THE WITCH'S DEN

Mrs Eastly was alone in the house. Cousin Mabel had gone and her twin stepsons had deserted her. Yes, deserted her. There was no other way to describe it and she knew by the look on their faces when they left the house, they would never come back to see her again.

She was sitting in the kitchen. There was no one to keep her company, but she did not feel lonely. Her heart was full of anger and hate, there was no space left in it for sadness or loneliness or anything else for that matter. Hatred for Cousin Mabel festered inside her. Mabel, she was sure, was the one behind it all. The more she thought about it, the more she was convinced that it was Mabel who had turned the twins against her. She made up her mind there and then that one day she would get her own back on her cousin, the commandant.

But first, Bertha had to concentrate her mind on catching those children in the village and deciding what she would do with them when she had got them. She could deal with the commandant later. Commandant indeed! One thing was for sure; she was going to defy the commandant's instructions

24

not to harm the children. She was absolutely determined to do that. And with those thoughts in her mind she began to feel quite confident and powerful again.

Mrs Eastly decided that she would be more comfortable and able to think things out more clearly if she were in the witch's den. So she went into the hall and turned one of the coat pegs from the upright position through 90 degrees until it was sitting sideways on. Instantly a secret panel slid open and she stepped into her den. She sniffed the stale air inside the room and sniffed again. She couldn't believe it. She simply couldn't believe it. "Children," she screamed. "Children have been here in my den!" She shook a fist. "I wouldn't like to be in their shoes when I find out their names, because when I do, I'll make them really suffer."

She walked round and round the room, all the while sniffing the air. "Boys – it's mostly boys – I can smell them," she said to herself. Then, holding back her head, she sniffed again. The scent from the boys seemed stronger higher up, so taking a chair she stood on it and sniffed the air near the ceiling. The scent was much stronger there. Strange. She sat down on the chair and tried to work out why that should be. She knew boys had been in her den but her imagination could not stretch far enough for her to envisage what had happened the day Alex and Ginger Tomkins had stumbled across her secret lair. And never, not even in a thousand years, would she guess that Alex Farroll had been pinned to the ceiling by one of her very own broomsticks! Long and hard though she thought, she couldn't fathom it out and in the end she gave up and started to ponder other things.

Deep in thought, she sat in the chair for a long time sifting through old memories. And then at last it came to her. The photographs of those two boys she had seen in the newspaper when she was in prison – they were the photographs of the boys who had helped to find Roman treasure on Tinsall Hill. She remembered their names: Ginger Tomkins and Alex Farroll. Alex Farroll, Alex Farroll, she mused. Then she remembered something else she had read in the newspaper, Alex had two sisters, one named Leanne and the other named Lindsey. Their photographs had been in the newspaper too, together with an account of how they had rescued a girl called Alison from a ditch into which her pony, Flicka, had thrown her. The witch cackled in triumph. They were the very same girls she and the twins had chased from Red House Farm on the day she and the boys had been arrested by the police. All she had to do now was to check the telephone directory for their addresses and the rest was easy. She rubbed her bony hands in glee.

But something kept nagging away at the back of Mrs Eastly's mind, warning her to be cautious, telling her not to act too soon. What was it? Then she remembered it was something Red Leader had reported to her when she came to see her in prison – robots! That was it – robot activity in the grounds, that's what Red Leader had reported. Then there was this article she had read in the newspaper about the dark side of the hill and how Jupiter, one of the robots, had flown the aliens back to Petranova. Mrs Eastly concluded that if the robots were clever enough to fly a spaceship – and single handed at that – back to another planet, then she must get rid of the one that remained whilst the other was away, otherwise she'd never get the children. Juno was the name of the robot that remained in the village. She knew where Juno worked and lived – Red Leader had tracked it there. A smile crossed the face of Witch Eastly. Satisfied with her plans, she reached for her spell book and fell fast asleep reading it.

CHAPTER FOUR

BROOMSTICK FLYING –
BACK TO BASICS FOR MRS EASTLY

Red Leader and Red One arrived early at Red House Farm the next day to find Mrs Eastly fast asleep in a chair in her den.

"Tallyho! Sister Bertha. Rise and shine. Your cousin Mabel has sent us. It's basic flying practise for you today." It was Red Leader who delivered the message.

Mrs Eastly opened sticky eyes and looked at Red Leader and Red One. They were carrying their helmets and goggles and dressed in full flying kit. They looked alert, they were slim, young and healthy – and they were smiling. Bertha caught a glimpse of herself in the mirror and groaned. What a contrast! She looked old, heavy, dull and miserable. She stood up, complaining of stiffness in her neck and legs as she prepared herself for training. Red One told her, not unsympathetically, that she shouldn't have slept all night in a chair. She said that her grandma had told her that bed was the best place to rest.

Mrs Eastly ignored her. She was secretly hoping that with a little luck and some hard work she might be competent enough to fly to Juno's workshop later on. For hours during the night she had studied her spell book and she was now confident that she could turn that clever bit of tin into a rusty bag of old nails. The thought amused her and almost brought a smile to her face.

Red Leader went outside, leaving Red One alone with Mrs Eastly.

"Are you sure you won't wear the flying kit we've brought you?" she said.

"Definitely not," came Mrs Eastly's curt reply.

Red One shrugged her shoulders. She ran her fingers across a rack of broomsticks.

"Which one would you prefer?" she enquired.

"Third from the left." Mrs Eastly hoped that the swiftness of her reply would make her appear knowledgeable, broomstick-wise.

Red One gave Mrs Eastly the broomstick, opened the door and went outside. Mrs Eastly followed.

Red Leader was waiting for them. "I want you to do one slow, simple circuit of the farmyard so we can make an assessment of what you can do and what you can't do. As I said, keep it simple, fly no higher than the house in case you get into difficulties. Take off when you are ready and we'll be waiting for you to do a nice gentle landing after you have completed the circuit. Now, before you take off is there anything you want to know? Have you any questions?" Red Leader asked.

Mrs Eastly shook her head, gave a strong push with her heavy legs and took off. She made a wobbly start and she was barely airborne before it became obvious she couldn't maintain a constant height. Her face looked strained and she bobbed up and down, up and down, as if she were riding a surfboard on a very choppy sea.

Red One began to feel anxious. "She's not in control. Her course is too erratic. She's not in control. She won't complete the circuit!"

But then Red Leader noticed the large water tank, almost full of water, standing in the middle of the farmyard, and she couldn't suppress a smile. "Splash landing coming up," she said, her smile broadening into an oversized grin.

Meanwhile, Mrs Eastly felt that her control of the broomstick was worsening and when she got to the bottom of one of her ups and downs she panicked and decided it was time to bale out. She jettisoned her broomstick directly over the large water tank and gave a loud shriek as her bottom struck the cold water.

When they pulled her out of the tank the witch was soaked to the skin. Mrs Eastly gulped air into her lungs and complained that she had never, in all her life, felt so cold and miserable. Red Leader ignored her complaints and made some notes in a training manual.

After allowing Bertha to change into some dry clothing, they kept her practising low-level circuits until five o'clock in the late afternoon. Red Leader said she was satisfied with the day's progress and made some more notes in her book. "Another couple of weeks and we'll have you right as rain," she said.

Bertha's face darkened at the word "rain" – she'd had enough of water for one day – and she directed an ugly look at her tutor.

Red Leader ignored it and said, "If you intend to do more flying after we've gone, keep it slow and keep it simple. Don't do anything fancy, okay? See you tomorrow then."

Mrs Eastly watched as Red Leader, followed by Red One, climbed away steeply, corkscrewing left, corkscrewing right, and then, after doing a loop-the-loop, she saw them settle down on a steady course for home.

She screamed and shook a fist after them. "Keep it slow, keep it simple. Don't do anything fancy. Dirty show offs – that's what you are." And as for Red Leader's comment that she was satisfied with the day's progress, she needn't have bothered. Mrs Eastly knew she had improved and she was very satisfied with her progress, very satisfied indeed. In fact, she was so full of confidence, she decided that she would visit Juno's workshop that very night and hit that squeaky piece of tin for six. "Strike while the iron's hot, that's my motto," she muttered to herself and stamped off into the house.

CHAPTER FIVE

MRS EASTLY CASTS A SPELL ON JUNO

Mrs Eastly had a rest after the afternoon's training. She waited until it was dark and then went outside to check the weather. The weather check was important. It was important because the humiliating experience of being hauled out of the water tank by Red Leader and Red One reminded her just how poor her flying capabilities were. She didn't want another ducking, so she checked visibility, cloud base and wind speed very carefully in order to make sure the conditions were something with which she could cope. She sighed with relief, conditions couldn't have been better – the flight was on!

She decided it was time to get ready, but not for one moment did she consider wearing the flying kit Red Leader and Red One had presented her with that morning. It was a cold night, so she started off by making sure that she wore plenty of woollies, and by the time she had finished putting on layer after layer, Mrs Eastly looked more bloated than ever. There was just one more thing she needed before going outside to face the cold night air.

It was her cloak. She rummaged around in her wardrobe and selected the warmest cloak she could find and into its deepest pocket she secreted a small golden box of magic dust. Satisfied, she looked at her reflection in the mirror. "Silly Bertha," she chided. "You've forgotten your hat!" Her pointed hat was lying on the bed. She put it on and tied the ribbon tightly under her chin. Looking at her image in the mirror again, she exclaimed, "That's better, Bertha, you look really lovely now," and she tightened the ribbon a little bit more, to make sure she wouldn't lose her hat in the slipstream.

Then a frown creased Mrs Eastly's forehead. She couldn't for the life of her remember the incantation or the actions she had to make to successfully cast a spell on Juno. She tried again. Try as she may, she couldn't even remember how the incantation started. Frustrated, she looked around and found the crumpled piece of paper onto which she had copied details of the spell, plus some added notes. She opened it up, spread it on the table, scanned it carefully, and then began to read out aloud:

With this magic dust and sign of the snake,
Into a bag of rusty old nails I thee make.

Notes: (1) After the words "With this magic dust" sprinkle the object/subject of the spell with the correct amount of magic dust, e.g. one, two or three pinches (see spell book).

(2) When reciting the words "sign of the snake" the letter "S" should be prescribed over the object/subject of the spell with the RIGHT hand.

WARNING: Failure to carry out these instructions carefully could produce unpredictable results that could prove dangerous to the person casting the spell.

That was scary! The warning that something nasty might happen to her if she got it wrong was scary. And the thought that she might end up as a snake, if she got it wrong – ugh! Now that was really scary. Mrs Eastly read and reread the spell and the notes until she had it all word perfect. She put the piece of paper in her pocket – just in case. Then she went outside again to make a final check on the weather. There was some cloud about, but it was high up, much higher than she intended to fly, so that was all right. There were plenty of gaps in the cloud for the moon to shine through and that pleased Bertha. If it had been very dark, or the visibility had been poor, her night navigation skills wouldn't have been up to it. But tonight, conditions were fair. Bertha mounted her broomstick and set course for Juno's workshop.

She took her time and flew very slowly.

Juno loved pop music. She was playing one of the latest tunes on the keyboard when the warning came. "Alert! Alert! Bandits approaching, range one mile, rooftop level. Alert! Alert! Estimated time of arrival, four minutes! Repeat, ETA four minutes. Alert! Alert!"

Juno abandoned the keyboard and moved quickly across the room to the radar visual display unit.

The witch's echo was there. It was moving slowly across the tube, the telltale letter "W" trailing after it made it easily identifiable and it was heading towards the workshop!

Juno opened the window as wide as it would go. She wanted to make it easy for Mrs Eastly to gain entry. Satisfied, she returned to the keyboard. Her mechanical fingers moved smoothly over the keys and by playing quietly, she could hear what was going on above the sound of her tune.

The piece she was playing was one of her favourites and her metal body moved and swayed gently to the music without making the tiniest squeak.

A muffled sound came from the window. It was Bertha. With her large bulk, she had managed to get her broomstick and thick black cloak all tangled up with the catch on the window. Juno saw her in the mirror. As she tried to disentangle herself Bertha's cloak flapped like the wings of a large black bat that had been caught in a trap. Juno had to make a great effort not to laugh.

After a struggle, Bertha freed herself from the mess she was in. She parked her broomstick against the wall, raised herself on her tiptoes and crept as quietly as she could, positioning herself directly behind the robot. Juno pretended she hadn't heard a thing. Her mechanical fingers moved lightly over the keys, producing the sweetest of sounds.

Mrs Eastly was purring with anticipation as she plunged her hand into the deep pocket of her cloak and took out the golden box that contained the magic powder. It all seemed so easy. Then she opened the lid and was instantly filled with doubt. Was it just one pinch of the magic dust, or two? There was no time to check her notes. The robot had stopped playing the keyboard, any second it could turn around and see her. And not for the first time that day Mrs Eastly was struck by panic – she decided to take a chance and make it one pinch and not two. She whispered the incantation so that Juno wouldn't hear, "With this incantation and sign of the snake…"

But Juno did hear and as soon as the witch began her

incantation, Juno pressed her special invisibility button. Now, totally invisible, she stood in a corner of the room, watching and waiting to see Mrs Eastly's reaction.

The reaction was slow in coming. For what seemed like ages the witch stood there with her mouth gaping wide open. She really couldn't believe that she had done it. But she had, the robot was no longer to be seen. Wasn't that proof enough? Of course it was. She'd done what she had set out to do! The rolls of fat on Mrs Eastly's body began to quiver and shake as she cackled and danced about the room in high glee. Then she began to sing as she danced. Her voice was cracked and tuneless. She sang a verse that sounded something like this:

I've got rid of Juno,
I've got rid of Juno,
Just a spell on the kids will end the show,
And cousin Mabel will never know.
Yes, a spell on the kids will end the show
And cousin Mabel will never know.

She stopped singing. Something was wrong. Something was missing and she knew what it was. She looked down on the floor. Where was it? Where was the bag of rusty old nails that the spell was supposed to have reduced Juno to? It was nowhere to be seen.

Juno, invisible in the corner, tried to restrain the sound that was about to escape from her lips. She placed a metallic hand over her mouth and almost succeeded, but not quite. A tiny chuckle escaped and revelling in its freedom, it bounced and reverberated around the room

Mrs Eastly heard it and felt afraid. "Who's there?" she called. "I distinctly heard you laugh." She tried to sound fierce. "I know you're there. Come out and show yourself. I dare you to show yourself."

No answer from Juno. Somehow she managed to keep quiet.

Mrs Eastly began to have doubts about the spell. She remembered the dreadful warning in the notes and she asked herself, should she have given it two pinches of magic powder instead of just one? And did she make the sign of the snake with her right hand or her left? She couldn't remember. Again she panicked and with her bony hands she felt her body all over to make sure she hadn't turned herself into a snake or something equally horrid. She hadn't. As far as she could tell, she was still the same old Bertha. Well, that was a relief, and she consoled herself with the thought that the spell had at least worked in part. It must have – it had got rid of Juno and what could be better than that?

She decided to call it a night and return to Red House Farm. Perhaps on the way home she would call at the Farroll's house and give the girls a fright. "Great idea, Bertha," she whispered to herself. "That's what I'll do." She eased herself through the window, straddled her broomstick and with a light push with her heels on the wall of the workshop, made a smooth take-off. That pleased her. She thought about Red Leader and Red One, and with false humour she called out, "Tally ho! Tally ho! Go! Go!" Oh dear, what a pity they couldn't be present to see her smooth take-off. Still, she'd done a good job by getting rid of Juno, so she consoled herself with the thought that you just can't have everything.

Something had awaked Leanne about the time Mrs Eastly had first entered Juno's workshop. She didn't know what it was, but she couldn't get back to sleep again. She got out of bed, went into her sister's bedroom and called out softly, "Are you awake, Lindsey?"

"Have been for a long time," Lindsey whispered, as her face appeared from under the sheets where she had been hiding. "Something woke me up, I was frightened so I pulled the sheets over my head. When I heard you come into the room, I thought it was old witch face coming to get me."

Leanne gave Lindsey a cuddle and she got out of bed. Together, they walked to the window and talked in whispers so that they wouldn't wake up the others. They looked out of the window. The moon had appeared from behind a large cloud, it lit up the sky and turned night into day. "Look," said Lindsey, pointing, "You can see Red House Farm quite clearly across the fields."

"I can see it," said Leanne. "And I wonder what old witch face is up to tonight?" Before Lindsey had time to reply, there she was at the window, old witch face, herself! Pointed hat, black cloak, hooked nose, there she was bobbing up and down on her broomstick outside their window. The girls were terrified and unable to speak. Leanne found Lindsey's hand searching for hers. She gripped it tightly and held on to it.

The witch looked at them through the glass in the window and showed her yellow teeth as she began mouthing some words. They listened. Lindsey thought she was trying to sing. But, there was no tune to it and because the window was closed it was difficult to hear the words, but she thought the words sounded something like this:

Juno's been sent to pastures new,
It's something you ought to know.
Erelong I'll be back and then watch out,
I'll do the same to you.

Satisfied she'd scared the girls, the witch felt that she had accomplished enough for one night. All this spell casting, flying and frightening people had given her a tremendous sense of power. But now the feeling was wearing off and she felt tired. All she wanted now was – bed. She spun round on her broomstick and headed for home.

Frightened, the sisters held on to one another tightly, but their eyes were still trained on the broomstick. It was flying in the direction of Red House Farm. In the bright moonlight they could see the broomstick quite clearly, flying not much higher than the treetops and moving very slowly.

Unknown to the girls, someone else was watching too. It was Juno. She was tracking the "W" trail all the way back to Red House Farm. Alert and poised by the radar tube, she was waiting for a signal. She didn't have long to wait. Suddenly a red light appeared on the tube and an artificial voice called out: "Activate now! Activate now!"

Juno reached out and pressed a button.

Leanne and Lindsey were still watching at their bedroom window when they saw a brilliant light illuminate the sky over Red House Farm. It was the broomstick bursting into flames and for a few brief seconds they saw Mrs Eastly clearly silhouetted against the fiery glow, trying desperately to abandon the blazing broomstick before it finally plunged into the ground.

The moon, as though afraid to witness the incident, hid behind some clouds and stayed there for quite a long time. While it remained there, the night became very dark.

Lindsey knew exactly what had happened. Controlling her voice to an excited whisper, she said, "It's Juno. She bugged and booby-trapped her broomstick. She's blown old witch face up!"

"I hope she's not too badly hurt," said Leanne, who hated any kind of violence. She was biting her lip and looking anxious. Unlike Lindsey, she felt rather sorry for Mrs Eastly.

"Leanne, don't worry. She's not hurt. Not her – she was flying too low for that. For all I care, Juno could have blown her all the way to Australia and that's the truth of it."

"We'll have to thank Juno for keeping an eye on us, for keeping us safe tonight," said Leanne. "That's the first thing we have do in the morning, Lindsey, okay?"

"Okay," said Lindsey.

"Goodnight then, Lindsey. You okay now?"

"Yep. Goodnight, Leanne."

Leanne went back to her room, climbed into bed and fell asleep straight away.

But Lindsey couldn't sleep. She closed her eyes and tried to forget about Mrs Eastly. A troubling thought had come into her head and it wouldn't go away. Old witch face would try to get her own back on the twins for leaving her, Lindsey was absolutely sure of it. What would she do to them? What would she do to Bill? Lindsey was still worrying about it when, finally, she fell into a troubled sleep.

When the broomstick had exploded, it had done so directly over the water storage tank in the farmyard and a weary Mrs Eastly dragged herself out of the tank for the second time within 24 hours. She left the broomstick's charred remains on the ground where they had fallen. Staggering into the house, she towelled herself dry and went to bed. All the clothes she possessed were now soaking wet. She would have to wear full flying kit the following day. She had nothing dry left to wear!

39

CHAPTER SIX

MRS EASTLY DEFIES THE COMMANDANT AND LANDS HERSELF IN TROUBLE

Red Leader and Red One arrived at Red House Farm the next morning and were surprised to find Mrs Eastly already up and waiting for them. They were even more surprised to see that she was wearing full flying kit.

Red Leader greeted her, "Well, aren't you the early bird and dressed in full plumage too." She laughed at her own little joke. She sniffed the air. It smelled stale. "Shall we go outside?" she said. "Fresh air will do us good."

As soon as they were outdoors Red Leader spotted the remains of the burnt-out broomstick. "Hello, hello, what have we here? Had a little accident, have we?"

Bertha was ready for the question. She replied, "I was practising a little flying last night, after you'd gone. Just around the farmyard, mind you – no further – and suddenly, for no reason, my broomstick burst into flames and I ended up in the water tank – again!"

"Aha! So that's why you're wearing full flying kit,"

said Red Leader. "All your other clothes must be soaking wet." She couldn't resist a smile.

Mrs Eastly scowled.

Red Leader poked and stirred the charred remains of the accident with her feet. She stooped, picked up a piece of the burnt-out broomstick and examined it closely before allowing it to fall back to the ground. Taking out a tissue from one of her many pouched trouser pockets she wiped the blackened bits of carbon and dirt from her hands. When that was done, she placed the soiled tissue in a dustbin and carefully replaced the lid, then she spoke, "Do you think we could go into your den, Bertha. I'd like to take a look at your broomsticks. With your permission of course."

Mrs Eastly nodded her assent.

When she had finished her examination, Red Leader said, "How long have you had these broomsticks, Sister Bertha?"

Mrs Eastly couldn't remember. "It was a long time ago," she mumbled. "But they were top of the range stuff then, I can tell you. They weren't cheap."

Red Leader handed one of the broomsticks to Red One. She said, "Take a look and tell me what you think."

Red One took the broomstick and examined it carefully. "Hmm. Old fashioned. But I'd say it's okay for Sister Bertha's day-to-day requirements."

"Take another look," said Red Leader, and she pointed to a couple of tiny marks on the broomstick. "What do you make of those?"

Red One took another look, taking more care over the examination this time. "Wow, it's incredible!" she exclaimed. "It took a real expert to do this, and that's for sure." She handed the broomstick back to Red Leader.

"What is it? What is it?" Mrs Eastly clamoured to be told.

"Your broomsticks, Sister Bertha. They've all been bugged and booby-trapped," said Red Leader. "Now who would want to do such a thing to you? More important, perhaps, who do you know who would be capable of doing such a thing?"

Mrs Eastly's mouth sagged open. She had already lied to Red Leader by telling her that the previous night's flying practise had been restricted to the farmyard area and she knew she would have to lie to her again. She had to. How on earth could she tell her the truth and tell her she'd visited Juno at her workshop, put a spell on her and made her disappear? No chance. The less said about that the better. Any talk about the robots could put an end to the revenge she had planned for the children in the village and she was not going to relinquish that plan.

"No," she replied to the question, sounding as innocent as she could. "I don't know who would want to do such a thing to me. And I don't know anyone who would be capable of doing such a thing, either."

Red Leader decided that what she had discovered was so important it had to be reported straight away to the commandant. Maybe she would grant permission for them to return with a replacement broomstick for Bertha, they would just have to wait and see.

Mrs Eastly waved them off. She was glad to see them go.

Back at base, Red Leader confessed her doubts about Mrs Eastly to the commandant and she told her bluntly, "I think she's lying," she said. "She knows more about those bugged broomsticks than she's letting on. Despite all your warnings, she's up to something. And it's something bad, Ma'am, I can tell."

"I think you're right," said the commandant. "It's those children in the village, she's blaming them for something she brought on herself. I can't – we can't – allow her to hurt those children, can we?"

"No Ma-am, we can't."

"Leave it with me. I'll deal with it," said the commandant firmly. She dismissed Red Leader and rang for her adjutant and gave her the following list of instructions:

(1) Red One to deliver a replacement broomstick to Red House Farm and return all other broomsticks to HQ for inspection.

(2) Two security guards to be despatched to Red House Farm. They will remain under cover and keep Mrs Eastly under surveillance by day and by night until further notice.

(3) Mrs Eastly to be placed under close arrest and the commandant informed immediately if she should harm, or be suspected of harming, the local children.

The adjutant was quick to reply when she read the list. "If there's any arresting to be done, the security guards will need your signature, Ma-am." She took out a piece of paper from her document case and handed it to her superior.

"You've got it," said the commandant, signing and returning the paper to her.

"Thank you Ma-am," said the adjutant, returning the signed document to her document case. She took her leave and left the office. She had work to do and it had to be done in a hurry.

Mabel paced up and down her empty office. The news delivered to her by Red Leader told her that the differences between herself and Cousin Bertha were coming to a head, and more rapidly than she had anticipated.

Only a restricted number of HQ staff knew that security guards were being despatched to Red House Farm on surveillance duties. Red One was not included in that number. Her instructions were to deliver the new broomstick and return with the old ones and take them to the research and development department at HQ.

She arrived at Red House Farm the next morning. "I see you're not wearing flying kit," she said, presenting Mrs Eastly with a new broomstick.

"It's more comfortable than that ridiculous outfit you want me to wear," Mrs Eastly replied curtly, and she took the new broomstick from Red One without a single word of thanks.

Red One didn't reply. She was getting used to Sister Bertha's rudeness. She merely shrugged her shoulders and got on with her task.

Mrs Eastly watched as Red One tied the old broomsticks into a bundle. When she had done that she slung them over her shoulder and made ready for her departure.

Bertha didn't want to delay Red One. In fact, the sooner she left, the better. It suited her plans, but she couldn't resist asking the question, "That bundle you're carrying, won't it make you tail heavy?"

"Well spotted, Sister Bertha," said Red One. "You're thinking like an aviator."

Mrs Eastly blushed at the compliment and felt sorry she'd been so rude. She said, "So, how will you deal with it then?"

"Nose heavy – body weight slightly back. Tail heavy – body weight slightly forward. Simple," she said. "Hang on for a minute, Sister Bertha, and I'll give you a little demo." She adjusted her weight on the broomstick, taking care to show Bertha how it was done. Then, with a push from her strong legs, she made a perfect take-off.

"What do you think of that then?" she said, after completing a perfect circuit and making an equally perfect landing.

Mrs Eastly was impressed. "That was terrific, Red One. And thanks for telling me how to do it. Red Leader couldn't have done it better." Her voice was unctuous with praise.

"Huh!" said Red One, "You don't have to tell me that. I know she couldn't."

There was an odd look in Red One's eyes as she spoke. Mrs Eastly recognised the look. She knew what it was. It was jealousy! Red One was jealous of Red Leader! Useful knowledge indeed, perhaps it would come in useful later. Putting her suspicions to the test, she replied, "Do you know, I think you're right about that Red One. You're every bit as good as Red Leader. I think you're better. And to tell the honest truth, I think you're *far* better." The overblown compliment was a deliberate attempt by Mrs Eastly to widen the wedge between Red One and Red Leader and to make it clear to Red One that she was on her side. And it worked!

Red One beamed and said sincerely, "Any problems, Sister Bertha, you know who to ask. I'll do my best to help."

The compliment had worked even better than Bertha expected. She'd made a hit with Red One, she could tell. And one day, you never know, Red One might make a very useful ally."

"Thanks for your offer to help, I'll keep that in mind," said Bertha and she gave Red One a cheerful wave as she took off. And she watched admiringly as Red One made a steep climbing turn that took her on course for HQ.

Mrs Eastly couldn't wait to try out the new broomstick. She examined it. The weight was different. It was much lighter than the ones she had been used to. She muttered a few words of magic and the broomstick flew out of her hands and flew around the farmyard, twisting and turning and gyrating wildly. "That's one bit o' magic I'll never forget," she muttered. She was thinking of the twins. "Abandoning me like that!" she snarled. "Ungrateful devils! I just wish they were here, that's all. I'd give them some surprises with this little beauty, I can tell you." She uttered a few more words of magic and the broomstick instantly obeyed. It returned and lay in the palm of her hands; it twitched for a few seconds and then became still and docile.

The new broomstick was slightly longer than the old ones. "Extra length – extra zip!" That's what Red One had told her. The witch took off and made a gentle turn around the farm. It felt good. So good in fact, she decided to continue with circuits and bumps, as Red Leader called them, until it got dark. Round and round she flew. One circuit for Ginger Tomkins and the next one for Alex Farroll, one for each of the boys she had smelled in her den. What should she do with them? Round and round she flew, trying to make up her mind.

Looking into the visual radar display unit, Juno observed the activity that was taking place at Red House Farm. She was puzzled by the absence of the telltale "W"s. She realized that it must be Mrs Eastly, but where were the "W"s? The answer came almost immediately. "They've found the bugs," she said to herself. "Well, there's plenty more where they came from." And she set out for Red House Farm, determined to rectify the matter.

When Juno reached the farm, the witch was still practising circuits and landings. In fact she had done so many, she was getting bored and wanted to try something different. She dismissed the advice that Red Leader had given to her earlier – not to try anything fancy – and listened instead to the tiny voice in her head that told her to loop-the-loop! Mrs Eastly hesitated. The voice in her head said, "Go on, Bertha, you can do it – it's easy!"

Juno, with her invisibility switch on, watched as Mrs Eastly dug her toes into the ground, gave a strong push and pointed the nose of the broomstick almost vertically skywards. The new broomstick responded magnificently. Bertha was now at least ten times higher than the highest tree when she started her loop. She drew in her breath. Too late she recalled Red Leader's warning that she should wear flying kit – especially when performing aerobatics. There was a magnetic strip on the broomstick onto which her flying suit trousers were designed to stick. It was there to keep her secure when doing difficult manoeuvres. But Bertha wasn't wearing flying kit, so she was not wearing the special safety trousers!

Too late now! Bertha was unseated as she turned over the top of the loop. She held onto the broomstick with her bony hands and threshed about with her heavy legs, trying to get them over the handle again. It was no good. Her efforts were in vain. Futile! The broomstick was in a nosedive and completely out of control. Bertha closed her eyes and waited for the impact. She landed, not in the water tank this time, but in the duck pond. She was lucky. The thick mud saved her from injury.

On her hands and knees Mrs Eastly crawled back to the farmhouse looking like a large black shiny slug and she left a trail of slime behind her. The broomstick floated to the edge of the pond where it lay, undamaged. It took Juno less than five minutes to implant another "W" bug into it, but she didn't booby-trap it this time; she felt that the witch had suffered enough for one day!

Satisfied, Juno returned to her workshop and her keyboard and soon she had filled the room with the sound of the latest pop music. The place was almost rocking when Leanne and Lindsey arrived and they had to shout above the music to thank Juno for keeping a protective eye on them the previous evening. Juno stopped playing the keyboard when Leanne told her that she was worried about Mrs Eastly. Leanne went on to describe to her how she and Lindsey had witnessed the witch struggling for dear life in the blazing flames of her broomstick just a few seconds before it crashed to the ground. Juno could see the grief in Leanne's face and she was quick to reassure her that the witch was okay. "When her broomstick exploded she landed in the water tank, Leanne. She got a ducking, but she's okay." She gave one of her little metallic laughs and Leanne sighed with relief. Juno didn't tell them about Mrs Eastly's latest mishap, the one that had landed her in the duck-pond!

In reply to a question from Lindsey, Juno told them that she considered Mrs Eastly had suffered enough and, that being the case, she had decided not to set up any more booby-traps to light up the night skies again. Lindsey was bitterly disappointed, but Leanne was relieved. No more explosions, the news was like music to her ears.

The sisters said goodbye to Juno and went to seek Alison and Laura. Leanne wanted to tell them about last night and how they saw old witch face bobbing up and down on her broomstick outside their bedroom window. Lindsey wanted to tell them that they'd seen Mrs Eastly's broomstick burst into flames and tell them about the explosion that had blown her sky high before she landed headfirst into the water tank!

She waited until later, when she was alone with Alison, to tell her that she was worried that Mrs Eastly might want to get her own back on the twins. When she did, Alison became anxious too.

Despite all her mishaps, Mrs Eastly was determined to carry out her threats against the children in the village. She decided to deal with the boys first. At precisely ten o'clock that night she retrieved her broomstick from the duck pond and set off in the direction of Ginger Tomkins' house. His window was wide open. She stood by his bed and looked down on him. He was fast asleep.

She took out the box containing the magic dust and began the incantation:

With this magic dust and sign of the snake
Into a ginger-haired mouse I thee make.

Instantly, poor Ginger disappeared and in his place, fast asleep on the pillow, there lay a tiny red-haired mouse! The witch picked up the mouse and popped it into a bag that was tied around her waist. She breathed into the bag and said, "Be patient, little mousy, you'll soon have a nice little friend to play with."

The witch didn't waste any time, she climbed out through the open widow and sped in the direction of Alex Farroll's house.

Alex liked fresh air and always slept with his window wide open, so the witch had no difficulty in getting into his room. She looked down on him, tousle-haired and fast asleep in bed. Taking out the golden box of magic dust, she began her incantation:

With this magic dust and sign of the snake
Into a fair-haired mouse I thee make.

Instantly, Alex disappeared and on his pillow lay a tiny fair-haired mouse. Mrs Eastly picked it up and popped it into the bag along with the other one. "There now," she said. "So, that's the two of you. I've got a lovely cage waiting for you on the kitchen table in Red House Farm and it's got a nice big wheel for you to play in. You can take it in turns to make it spin. The faster you run, the faster it will go. See who gets tired first. You'll love it. You'll really have fun." She bared her yellow teeth. "Then, after that, there's a special treat in store for you. But more about that later."

She secured the bag containing the mice round her waist, climbed out of the window and sped towards Red House Farm.

Juno had seen the telltale "W" marks on the radar screen leaving the houses of both boys and was at Red House Farm waiting for Mrs Eastly to arrive. She saw the commandant's two security guards hiding in the shadows outside Mrs Eastly's kitchen window and guessed why they were there. With her invisibility switch on, Juno joined them and waited patiently for the witch to appear.

Mrs Eastly arrived and went into the kitchen. The two guards moved from their hiding place. They didn't hear the tiny mechanical squeak that came from Juno's legs as she joined them. They watched Mrs Eastly's movements through the kitchen window.

Mrs Eastly was very excited. Her bony hands were trembling as she struggled to untie the leather bag that was fastened around her waist. At last she released it and tossed the bag onto the table alongside a wire cage. She opened the door of the cage and tested the wheel that hung inside it. It spun around smoothly, making only the slightest whirring sound. This pleased the witch. She cackled and tested it again. "Oh yes, my little beauties, you'll have a nice time tonight, playing on this." She opened the leather bag, took out the two frightened mice and threw them into the cage. She poked at them before closing the door, saying, "You boys are the first. I'll get the girls tomorrow. Nothing can stop me now – nothing!" And she laughed and laughed until she could hardly breathe.

She went to a cupboard, opened the door and pulled out a large black cat from the dark recess into which it had been so cruelly imprisoned. The poor animal was frightened and struggled in vain to get free. Gripping it firmly in her bony hands the witch thrust it towards the cage and the two mice cowered away, squeaking in terror. "There, there," she said. "There's no need for that. I'm going to let you have a nice time playing with the wheel tonight. Then in the morning it's my turn to have some fun and pussy here's going to help me, aren't you pussy?" Again the poor cat struggled, but failed to release itself from her grip. "Tomorrow, we're going to play a little game called 'hide and seek'. It's going to be great fun and this is how we're going to play it. First, I release you from the cage so you can run away and try to hide and then after the count of three I release pussy and let him try to find you…"

But by now, the guards had seen and heard enough. They burst through the kitchen door and placed Mrs Eastly under close arrest. One of the guards produced a witch's mobile phone (WMP) and spoke directly to the commandant.

Juno, with her invisibility button pressed, stood in the corner of the room and watched the proceedings.

Mrs Eastly was defiant to the last. She screamed threats at the guards, "You fools, release me, or it will be the worse for you."

One of the guards spoke to her roughly, and told her to sit down and be quiet.

Mrs Eastly ignored her. "My turn will come and I'll get the two of you," she yelled. Then to the one who had told her to sit down and be quiet, she said, "As for you, no matter how long it takes, I will make you feel sorry for the way you talked to me just now. Just wait and see if I don't."

She had no time to say any more. The commandant swept into the room escorted by several officers. She wore striped epaulettes on her shoulders and had lots of gold leaf on her helmet to denote her rank. Her officer escort parked their broomsticks neatly against the wall. They were the very latest military broomsticks, very powerful and very fast.

The commandant didn't waste any time. She barked out some orders. Two of her officers were instructed to take the mice back to their respective bedrooms and there, change them back into human form. "Make sure they do not remember any of tonight's events," she commanded. The two officers saluted; they left the room, taking the cage and the two mice in it away with them.

The black cat managed to free itself from Mrs Eastly's grip; it ran away and escaped into the night.

Juno didn't interfere. She followed the two officers with the mice in the cage to make sure the commandant's instructions were properly carried out, not leaving them until she saw that Alex and Ginger were lying peacefully asleep in their beds again. Meanwhile, Mrs Eastly was taken away to ride in tandem with one of the officers. She noted, with a certain amount of satisfaction, that the officer adjusted her position on the broomstick to compensate for the extra weight – just as Red One had demonstrated, earlier.

The commandant used her WMP to communicate with her adjutant and gave her a brief outline of what had taken place. The adjutant assured her that the charge sheets would be raised straight away so that proceedings could go ahead first thing in the morning. The commandant thanked her and in a weary voice wished her goodnight.

Arriving at HQ, she retired to her room, flung herself on her bed fully clothed and tried to sort out in her mind all the evidence concerning her cousin Bertha's trial that was to be held the following morning.

Next morning, Mrs Eastly awoke in her bed to find Red One in her cell with a cup of tea. "I can't stay, Sister Bertha," she whispered. "And I'm not supposed to speak to you. But please take my advice and say that you will accept the commandant's punishment when they charge you this morning. On no account elect for trial by court martial. Please…" And before Bertha could question her she left the cell and locked the door behind her.

Mrs Eastly took Red One's advice and agreed to accept the punishment awarded by the commandant. She was given a six-month sentence to be served in Bleak Court, a witches' correction centre situated on Black Rock, a small island off the southern tip of the Lleyn Peninsula.

Mrs Eastly groaned when she heard the sentence being read out. She knew that a tough time lay ahead of her.

As they were leading Mrs Eastly away to serve her sentence, Red One managed to secrete a WMP into one of the pockets in Mrs Eastly's cloak without being observed. In the not too distant future, this one single act would dramatically change the lives of many and neither Red One nor Mrs Eastly would escape the consequences.

CHAPTER SEVEN

BLEAK COURT ON BLACK ROCK

Mrs Eastly's room was situated on the top floor of Bleak Court. She had to climb three flights of stone stairs to reach the top landing and a maid, who informed her that in half an hour she was finished work for the day, showed her to her room.

Mrs Eastly paused to draw breath before opening the door and made a silent vow to try and lose a few pounds during her stay on Black Rock. All that weight she was carrying and all those stairs, little wonder she felt worn out!

The door wasn't locked. She opened it and entered the room. The maid followed. The room was small, but it had a large window that stretched from ceiling to floor, the glass on the outside was streaked with rain. Bertha wiped away a film of moisture from the inside pane and peered out. Immediately below and surrounded by a high wall was a cobbled courtyard. The rain on the cobbles made them shine as if they had been polished. Raising her gaze and looking over the wall Mrs Eastly was treated to an outstanding view of the Welsh coast and the mountains beyond. The view was magical, there was no other way to describe it – and you didn't have to look through the eyes of a witch to appreciate such breathtaking beauty! Reluctantly, Bertha turned away from the window to take stock of her room. The contrast between the glories of what she had seen and the wretchedness of what she was looking at now could not have been more marked! In one corner of the dingy room there was a cracked hand basin; it had two taps, one of them leaked. Drip! Drip! Mrs Eastly instructed the maid to get someone to fix it – today! The maid said she would and took the opportunity to leave the room. Mrs Eastly continued to look around.

In another corner of the room stood a battered old wardrobe and set against the wall, opposite the window, was a single bed with a rickety chair placed on either side of it. Mrs Eastly felt the bed. It was hard. She noted the badly frayed mat that lay at the side of the bed. There was no other furnishing she could see in the room.

Bertha slipped off her shoes and stood on the mat. For all the difference it made they needn't have bothered with it at all; the cold from the stone floor came up through the worn threads and made her feet feel damp, as well as cold!

She lay on the hard bed to reflect on the events that had taken place over the past 24 hours. Reflect? No chance. Images of her cousin, the commandant, came into her mind and wouldn't go away. Actually, Bertha didn't mind that at all. In fact, once the images were there, she encouraged them to stay. They helped her stoke up further the hatred she already felt for her cousin. There was no doubt about it, Mrs Eastly hated Cousin Mabel and she hated her with all of her being. Mabel was the cause of all this misery. She'd poisoned the minds of the twins and made them turn against her and now she was telling her how she, Bertha, should run her life. The cheek of it! Well, she wouldn't be allowed to get a way with it and Bertha was the one to see that she didn't. But it was a case of doing first things first; she couldn't do everything at once. So, Mrs Eastly put her desire for revenge against the children in the village to the back of her mind; she would wait and deal with them later, after she had first taken care of her cousin.

She then decided two things: Number one, she wasn't going to stay and serve out her six-month's prison sentence on Black Rock. She was absolutely determined about that! Somehow, she would find a means of escape. Just how, she didn't know. Well, not yet, but given just a little time she knew that she could devise a plan. And number two, after she'd escaped – and this was the important bit – she was confident that she could raise a force against the commandant, fight and defeat her. With the defeat of the commandant, the New Order would topple with her and the Old Order would be restored. Bertha sighed with relief at the thought of it. And it wasn't because she wished to adopt the commandant's mantle when she fell. Oh dear, no, that was the last thing she wanted. Personal power and authority did not interest Mrs Eastly in the slightest. She was a lazy person; personal power and authority needed hard work and tireless activity, should one have the wish to keep it. Bertha knew that and hard work and tireless activity was something she was not prepared to give. All she wanted was for things to go back to the way they were before, so that she could say and do what she liked, when she liked – and no questions asked!

It had been a long and tiresome day, she was tired out; she undressed, slipped between the sheets and slept.

When she reported for breakfast at seven the next morning there was only one thing on Mrs Eastly's mind, escape from Bleak Court on Black Rock. That was her number one priority!

The maid who had showed her to her room the previous night was there to greet her. She was full of apologies and said, "My name's Martha, Mrs Eastly. I meant to tell you last night. But I wanted to get that faulty tap in your room sorted out and it made me forget."

"Oh yes. What's happening about the tap?" Bertha asked, making her voice sound friendly.

"The man's fixing it now. Sorry, Mrs Eastly, he couldn't do it yesterday." The maid waited for Bertha to express her annoyance.

But Bertha did no such thing. On the contrary, she gave the maid the sweetest smile she could muster and said, "That's alright, Martha, my dear, don't worry your pretty little head about it. After all, it's only a tap."

For a second the maid looked relieved, then she said timidly, "Thanks, Mrs Eastly, but there's something else I have to tell you."

"Then fire away, Martha," said Bertha, keeping her voice as pleasant as she knew how.

Martha said, "It's about your breakfast, Mrs Eastly. You have to cook your own breakfast and wash up your dishes afterwards. You'll get a cooked lunch and dinner, but you have to help with the washing up. I'm ever so sorry, but those are the rules."

The girl had a lovely soft Southern Irish accent and listening to her speak was like listening to music, at least that's what Bertha thought. She replied and said, "That's alright, Martha, 'rules is rules' as they say. And please, please don't worry about it, because I'm not." And she bared her teeth into what she thought was a pleasing smile. The scheming old witch was being charming for a reason, she needed a friend in the enemy camp. Poor Martha didn't know it, but already she'd been marked down by Bertha as the one most likely to fit the role. Mrs Eastly was satisfied that after a spot of grooming she and the girl would get along just fine!

Martha had been expecting an angry outburst from Mrs Eastly when she told her about her chores and it came as a pleasant surprise to find her so co-operative. In fact, Mrs Eastly had behaved with great charm and understanding about the whole business. Martha thought that perhaps Mrs Eastly wasn't as bad as the rumours made her out to be.

A sullen-faced prisoner sidled up and sat down beside Bertha at the breakfast table and tried to engage her in conversation. Bertha didn't like the look of her, so she ignored her completely and ate her breakfast in silence. When she had finished eating and washed up her dishes, Mrs Eastly looked at the lesson timetable that hung on the dining room wall. She shuddered when she read the titles of some of the subjects that were on the list: citizenship, administration, cookery, cleaning, gardening, broomsticks – care and maintenance of. Mrs Eastly stared hard at that one and read it again. Broomsticks – care and maintenance of? She thought that was a laugh! She couldn't resist it – no one was looking – so she took out her pen and after the words "Broomsticks – care and maintenance of" she added the words "optional exercise – broomstick flying and escape tactics!!"

As Mrs Eastly walked away from the notice board, she felt that she had successfully completed her first act of defiance at Bleak Court on Black Rock. She was smiling to herself at the thought that what she had done was only the beginning; the real stuff was yet to come!

Bertha and the other sullen-faced inmate assembled with other prisoners in the library, where they were awaiting the arrival of the governor/tutor. She got the surprise of her life when she appeared. She had expected to be confronted by some sort of an ogre. A tough looking sort of "you play ball with me and I'll play ball with you" type of woman, sprouting hair on chin and top lip. But the woman who entered the room wasn't like that at all. She was young, and she was very beautiful. She dazzled them with a gentle smile, saying good morning to them all, individually. That was how Bertha discovered that the name of the sullen-faced woman who had sat beside her at breakfast was Mrs Fairfax.

The beautiful young woman began to speak. "My name is Megan, Megan Roberts and I'm the governor of Bleak Court and your tutor…" Her introductory address lasted for about ten minutes and she ended her talk by saying, "I sincerely hope that your visit here will be happy and to our mutual benefit."

"Happy? Mutual benefit? You must be joking!" Mrs Eastly muttered quietly.

Bertha didn't pay much attention to the lecture on citizenship, she had no interest in that, whatsoever. But she was interested in the person who delivered the lecture, Megan Roberts. She looked no more than a young girl of 20 and her black hair hung down past her shoulders, shining like silk. She smiled frequently during her talk and Mrs Eastly couldn't help thinking that her teeth would put the whitest of pearls to shame. Mrs Eastly said to herself – and not without a pang of jealousy – that Megan Roberts was the loveliest woman she had ever seen.

Most of the rest of the day seemed to have been spent digging in the garden and sowing vegetable seeds of some kind or other. To her surprise, Mrs Eastly enjoyed working with the spade and she thought, with regret, about how much she had neglected her own garden at Red House Farm.

The day ended where it had begun, in the library. And when five o'clock came, Megan Roberts announced it was "free time" until first lecture the following day. Once again Mrs Fairfax tried to make conversation, but once again Bertha turned her back on her and ignored her completely. Bertha left the library, intending to have a little lie down before her evening meal. One thing she'd learned about gardening – it was very tiring!

Outside the door of her room she met Martha, the maid. "Hello, Martha," she said. "Would you like to come in, have a little chat?"

"That's fine, to be sure," Martha replied. "It's time for my break and I am allowed to speak to the…"

"Prisoners," said Bertha, helping her out.

Martha smiled. Her teeth were white, almost as white as the governor's.

Bertha caught a glimpse of her own yellow teeth in the mirror and it made her feel quite miserable. But she didn't stay miserable for long. She had other things on her mind. There were questions to be asked and answers to be given and Martha might just be the one with the answers.

Bertha sat her down in one of the rickety old chairs. She took a pillow from her bed, patted it and fluffed it up and suggested to Martha that it might make her more comfortable if she placed it as a support for her back. The maid refused, but her heart warmed towards Mrs Eastly for making the kind offer and she thanked her most profusely. Bertha could tell by the look in Martha's eyes that she liked her and it was then that she knew that her plan to make

Martha her ally in the enemy camp was definitely going to work.

Mrs Eastly opened the conversation. "I really like the governor. She's very pleasant, isn't she?"

"She is that," replied Martha in her soft Irish voice, adding, "and she's very kind too. She's one of the kindest persons I've ever met."

"Praise indeed. And in what way is she kind to you, Martha?" questioned Mrs Eastly, sweetly.

"Ooh! You know, in lots and lots of ways. Just now, she's teaching me business studies. And in two year's time, I'll have saved up enough money to buy Mr Murphy's shop in Ballinasloe." She blushed. "Then I can get married to my boyfriend, Joseph."

Interesting though this was, Bertha could not see how it would fit in with her plans to escape. She tried a different tack and said, "But it's so sad, isn't it. The governor. What sort of a life is there here, I mean, for a beautiful young woman like that?"

Martha smiled, a secret sort of a smile. Bertha's question set her off gossiping and she didn't stop for over half an hour. Then, stopping as abruptly as she had started, she stood up, said she had overstayed her welcome, that her break time was over and that she had work to do before dinner. Bidding Mrs Eastly goodbye, she left the room.

Mrs Eastly did not have the opportunity to speak to Martha again that evening. She retired early to bed to ponder over all the interesting things Martha had chatted about, things Bertha wanted to dwell on.

The witch lay on the bed, going over in her mind what Martha had told her. She went over and over it again, enjoying the sound of Martha's voice, so calm and soothing, and she thought about the governor, Megan Roberts.

The surprising fact revealed by Martha's chatter was that Megan Roberts was not leading a lonely miserable life on Black Rock. On the contrary, she was leading a very happy social life, plenty of parties, lots of friends – including boyfriends!

"But how? How could that be?" Bertha had asked. "I mean, you know – we're miles away from civilisation here. Cut off from everything."

Martha had given her another one of her secret smiles and she spoke confidingly to Bertha, "Her brother is a sorcerer and lives with the rest of their family in a mountain castle on Cader Idris. She goes there a lot. Parties and dances and concerts, there's always something happening there."

Bertha couldn't prevent the crafty look that crossed her face when she said, "But how does she get there?" She gave a little laugh. "Surely not by broomstick?"

"You can see for yourself," said Martha. "Tomorrow night, you can see for yourself how she gets to meet her family. Tomorrow night her brother is coming to take her to his birthday party at the castle on Cader Idris. Ten o'clock tomorrow night look out of that big window. Look out across the bay. Look out to the high peak in the mountains and you'll see him. He always comes that way."

Bertha fell asleep quite contentedly that night, dreaming of castles and moonlit mountains.

The next day could not go quick enough for Mrs Eastly. She kept looking at her watch. Once she caught Megan doing the same thing! As the time drew close to five o'clock she noticed that a sparkle had come into Megan's eyes. Clearly she was looking forward to her brother's birthday party.

When free time was announced, Bertha mounted the stairs to her room; already they felt easier to climb. In the corridor, before she arrived at her door, she met Martha. The meeting was no accident. Martha had not spoken a single word to anyone all day, except in response to orders. Feeling lonely, she had decided to lay in wait for her new friend, Mrs Eastly, and was delighted when she was invited into her room for a chat.

Bertha tried to get Martha to say more about the meeting between Megan and her brother, but she would not be drawn. All Martha would say was, "Look out of that big window at ten o'clock. Look out to the high peak."

Having failed on that one, Bertha decided to bite the bullet and go for the big one – escape! And in a voice sounding as nonchalant as she could make it, she said, "You know, Martha, it surprises me that no one has ever tried to escape from Black Rock."

This time Martha did respond and she said sadly, "Oh, but they did. But nobody tries to escape from Black Rock anymore. It's far too dangerous."

"Too dangerous! How? Why?"

"Because all those who try to escape end up dead, that's why," said Martha. She looked thoroughly miserable; it was obvious she wanted to drop the subject.

But that didn't suit Mrs Eastly. She wanted to know more, so she tried humour, "You're having me on, I know you are," and she gave a little laugh. "You are, Martha, aren't you? I mean – you know – everybody ending up dead – it's a joke, isn't it?"

Bertha's little trick question worked. "No, I'm not joking, Mrs Eastly," said Martha, "I've witnessed two such attempts and they both failed." The troubled expression was still on her face.

It was clear that Martha didn't want to go on and for a moment or two Mrs Eastly hesitated. But determined to find out more, she persisted with her questions. "What happened? What is it that's made you look so sad, Martha?" Bertha asked gently. They were standing at the big window. She was holding Martha's hand and they were gazing out to sea.

For a while, looking like two statues, they stood there silently and then Martha began to speak. Hesitantly and slowly she began. "That first time, that first attempt, there were five witches held captive in Bleak Court. One day, one of the witches said she couldn't stand it any more and said she was going to escape." Martha stopped talking; clearly it was an effort for her to go on.

Bertha persisted. She said gently, "Was she serious, I mean, about trying to escape?"

"Oh yes," said Martha, "With the help of the others she broke down that wooden gate in the high wall and they all rushed towards the cliffs and the sea. They were heading for those rocks over there." She pointed to the spot. "I was walking on those rocks, and when I saw them coming towards me, I hid. They stopped close by me and I could hear every word that they said."

"Can you remember what they said?" Bertha asked.

"How could I ever forget? Mrs Blackstone, for that was the name of the woman who was determined to escape, said she was going to swim across the bay. Said that when she reached the other side she would go to some friends and they would hide her and look after her."

"Sounds crazy to me. It's too far to swim across the bay," said Mrs Eastly.

"That's what I thought. That's what the others thought. They tried to persuade her not to try. They said it was too far to swim and the sea too cold and that she'd never make it. That's what they told her."

"And what did Mrs Blackstone say to that?"

"She said, 'If I were a fish, I could.'"

"A fish!" exclaimed Bertha.

"A fish! Yes, that's what she said. Her friends thought she was crazy and told her so. She ignored them and spoke to the two who were standing closest to her. 'You two,' she said, 'take my arms and hold them fast.' They hesitated. 'Go on, do as I say.' She said it in a loud voice, so they did. Then she turned and asked the other two to take hold of her legs and they did. 'Now then,' said Mrs Blackstone, 'I want you to pick me up and throw me off this high place and into the sea. Take heed, because before I strike the water, you'll witness the strongest magic you've ever seen – this I do solemnly promise.'"

"And did they do as she asked, did they throw her into the sea?" There was a catch in Bertha's throat when she spoke.

"Yes, and from my hiding place I could see her body falling, falling, twisting and turning on its way down to the sea. Then, just before she struck the water, there was a bright flash of light and she changed into a fish." Martha's face had grown paler than ever, she seemed to be on the verge of tears.

Mrs Eastly handed her a tissue. She waited until she had finished dabbing her eyes, then she said, sympathetically, "What was it, Martha, what happened next?"

"Oh, it was horrible, just horrible, Mrs Eastly," said Martha. "With that bright flash of light Mrs Blackstone changed into a fish. But before it had time to disappear beneath the waves, a much bigger fish appeared and gulped it down. We never saw, or heard from Mrs Blackstone again." Martha made her way to the door, she was weeping and dabbing her eyes with the tissue.

Mrs Eastly called after her. "I'm sorry, Martha. Sorry you are so upset. Perhaps those escape stories are too much for you, my dear. Maybe you shouldn't go on with them?"

"No, no, that's alright, Mrs Eastly. I want to talk to you about them. You're my friend and it helps me. But if you don't mind I'll tell you about the other one some other time, tomorrow night, perhaps." And with that she left, closing the door behind her.

Hardened woman though she was, Martha's story about Mrs Blackstone's attempt to escape made her feel sorry; not so much for the poor woman, but for herself. It left a pang of fear in her breast and a warning message in her head, warning her that perhaps it was too dangerous to try and escape from Black Rock, after all?

Mrs Eastly didn't switch on the light in her room as the night darkened. In the fading light she sat in one of the rickety old chairs in front of the big window and thought again about Mrs Blackstone. Her solemn boast that they were about to witness the strongest magic had come true; she really did turn herself into a fish! But what happened afterwards, when a bigger fish gobbled her up, surely that was a wicked and cruel act of fate? It certainly made Bertha think. She thought long and hard about it. Finally, she came to the conclusion that dabbling in magic and casting spells was a very, very dangerous game to play. Just one tiny mistake or an unforeseen change of events and you could end up being far worse off than the intended victim. It was true. Mrs Blackstone, for example, when she changed herself into a fish; never, not in her wildest dreams, did she foresee that a much bigger fish would come along and gobble her up, now did she?

Events! Events! Mrs Eastly began to reflect about and bemoan her own recent trials and tribulations. All that spell casting on Juno and those boys in the village, what good had that done, and where had that got her? It had done her no good at all and landed her right here in Bleak Court on Black Rock. And who was to blame for all that? Not she, not Bertha. It was Cousin Mabel's fault. Of course it was!

Bertha looked at the luminous dial on her watch. It was almost ten o'clock. She dismissed all thoughts about Mrs Blackstone and cleared everything else from her mind. She was going to see something special. That's what Martha had told her.

She stared intently out of the window. No rain. The moon shone on the trees outside the courtyard, there wasn't a breath of wind and their branches did not stir.

Bertha stiffened in her chair. She saw something approaching in the distance. It was a white object with the high peak directly behind it and it was moving at great speed towards the tiny isle of Black Rock directly in line with her window.

Before it reached the high wall that surrounded Bleak Court the object had slowed down considerably and Bertha could make out what it was. It was a great, white-winged horse, its flanks glistening in the moonlight, its head straining at the reins. Sitting in the saddle, splendidly dressed was Megan's handsome brother. The horse landed gracefully in the middle of the courtyard and folded its wings.

Before the rider had time to dismount, Megan ran out to greet him. Her brother reached down and swooping her up, he set her down in the saddle just in front of him.

The horse galloped forward and then, with one beat of its powerful wings, it cleared the high wall. The sorcerer's black velvet cloak, edged with pure gold, flowed majestically behind him as horse and riders soared swiftly towards the high peak and the castle of Cader Idris.

Soon, they were out of sight. Bertha vacated the chair in front of the window. She couldn't be bothered to return it to where it belonged. She felt sorry for herself left behind in her miserable grey room in Bleak Court. She slumped down on her bed and before she fell asleep she tried to remember the last birthday party to which she had been invited. There hadn't been a last, or even a first birthday party to which she had been invited. In fact, she realized she hadn't been invited to any, not ever! Poor Bertha, for the life of her, she couldn't understand, why.

"Well," said Martha, the following evening, when she arrived for what had become their regular evening chat, "Well, did you see them?"

"I did," answered Bertha.

"And the horse with the wings, what did you think about all of it?" Martha's cheeks were flushed with excitement.

"It was a sight I'll never forget," said Mrs Eastly, truthfully.

"She didn't get back 'til five this morning, you know. I don't know how she does it."

"Neither do I," agreed Bertha. "At lectures and all day, she was as fresh as paint."

They were sitting on the side of Mrs Eastly's bed, facing the window. "I know," replied Martha. "To look at her, you'd think she'd had a good night's sleep."

Mrs Eastly eased herself from the bed and moved her bulk across the room to the window. Martha followed. They stared out of the window.

Mrs Eastly changed the subject. "You were going to tell me about that other thing. You know, about that other woman who tried to escape."

Martha's face fell. Bertha noticed and said, "You don't have to talk about it, Martha, not if it upsets you, you don't." Bertha was cunning; she knew exactly what to say, and how to say it, to persuade Martha to open up.

"Oh, that's alright, Mrs Eastly. You're my friend. Friends tell each other things. A trouble shared – you know…"

"I know. I know. That's what friends are for," said Mrs Eastly, unctuously. "So, what happened to her, Martha, what happened to that woman?"

Martha pointed her finger. "I was sweeping up, down there in the courtyard, just below this very window. Suddenly, Mrs Johnson appeared, brandishing the governor's broomstick. Laughing and waving it about, she was. The other prisoners appeared; they could tell that something dramatic was going to happen. They laughed and cheered and egged her on. They were shouting, 'Good old Johnny. Good old Johnny.' Mrs Johnson was very popular, you know. All the prisoners called her Johnny."

"What happened next? And how did she manage to get hold of the governor's broomstick?" asked Bertha. She waited with baited breath for Martha's reply. Perhaps the answer would provide Bertha with the means of escape she was seeking?

Martha explained how it had happened. "The governor, not this one, the one before, always used her personal broomstick when giving the lecture on 'Broomsticks – care and maintenance of'."

Bertha couldn't help smiling when she recalled what she had added to the notice hanging up in the dining room.

"And after her lecture, and at the end of the day," Martha continued, "she always locked her broomstick in a cupboard and took the key with her. Except, on that day, she forgot. She left the key lying on the table and went away without it. Mrs Johnson saw it and took it. Next thing, she was down in the courtyard and waving the broomstick about, like I told you."

"What happened next?" probed Mrs Eastly.

"Her fellow prisoners were becoming more and more excited. They started to sing and chant 'Fly Johnny! Fly Johnny! Go! Go! Go!' and she did. She climbed to a height almost twice as high as this building and then she swooped down and flew round and round the courtyard yelling in triumph before heading for the mainland. Then everything started to go wrong." Martha was looking into the distance; her face was as white as a sheet. In her mind's eye she was seeing what had happened to Mrs Johnson, all over again.

"What happened? Did she escape?" Bertha asked.

Martha replied, sadly. "I told you, nobody escapes from Black Rock. Poor Johnny, she twisted and turned in every direction to try and find an escape route to the mainland. It was no good, in every direction she flew, incredible gale force winds sprang up and forced her back to the courtyard."

"But there has to be a safe route out, there has to be," said Bertha.

"If there is, Mrs Johnson couldn't find it. And another thing," said Martha, "Johnny didn't know it. And neither did we, not 'til after."

"And what was that?" Bertha asked.

"The broomstick," said Martha. "It was programmed especially for one person and one person only to fly. No prize for guessing who that was!"

"The governor," Bertha found herself saying.

"Right," said Martha. "And the last time Mrs Johnson was forced back over the courtyard, the broomstick suddenly went berserk. It spun, it dived and it climbed again and began to spin. It spun so violently it made Mrs Johnson dizzy. She fell off the broomstick and dashed her head on the cobbles below. Her friends rushed to her aid, but it was no good. When they got to her, poor Johnny was stone cold dead."

The memory of Mrs Johnson's fate had upset Martha. She stopped talking and lapsed into silence.

Mrs Eastly was also upset. Not so much over the death of Mrs Johnson, oh dear, no. She was upset because the prospects of escape from Black Rock seemed to be getting less and less with the passage of every day.

Martha began to talk again. "They buried her in the courtyard," she said. "If you look around when you're down there, somewhere, at the edge of all those cobble stones, you'll come across a flagstone with a broomstick and the name 'Johnny' etched on it. That's where poor Johnny lies."

Mrs Eastly wasn't affected in the least by what she had heard. What had happened to poor Johnny didn't mean a thing to her. She didn't care a jot. But she had to say something sympathetic because Martha was waiting for a response. At last she managed to say, "Oh dear, how very sad,"

Martha nodded her head. "Yes, it was sad. We were all crying at the funeral."

Deep down in her bones, Bertha felt there was something odd about the story concerning the key. She smelt a rat. She said, "How could the governor have been so careless – you know, leaving the key on the table?"

"She did it on purpose," said Martha, her voice rising in anger. "It all came out in the enquiry. She said she was bored, that she was only playing a game. Said it was all a dreadful accident and not for a minute did she think that Mrs Johnson would get hurt, and as for being killed – never! What a liar! I saw the cruel smile that crossed her face when she knew that poor Johnny was dead."

She said she was only playing a game. That's what the governor had said. It was only a game she was playing with Mrs Johnson. It reminded Mrs Eastly of something. It reminded her of the "cat and mouse" game she had planned for the boys in the village, that night she had them caged up as mice in the kitchen, the night she was caught and arrested by Mabel. It occurred to her that she and the previous governor shared something in common. Bertha did not have to think very hard to work out exactly what that was. She already knew. She said to Martha, "The governor, she must have had a terribly cruel streak in her nature, to do what she did to poor Johnny. Tell me, what happened to her next, what happened after the enquiry was over?"

"It was the New Order who led the enquiry," said Martha. "They found her guilty and banished her to a secret isle even more remote than Black Rock. Banished for life, so she was. And that's how we came to get Megan Roberts. She's of the New Order. She's lovely." Martha was smiling when she said it.

Bertha didn't reply, she was thinking about the attempted escapes and how they had gone so terribly wrong.

Martha left the window and made for the door. She stopped at the bed, took up a bundle of newspapers and handed them to Bertha. "I brought these for you. Thought you might like to catch up on all the outside news. Same time tomorrow, Mrs Eastly?"

"Yes, Martha," said Bertha, wearily. "Same time tomorrow." She closed the door after Martha and laid the newspapers on one of the rickety chairs, promising herself that she would have a quiet read in bed before going to sleep.

She snuggled down under the blankets with the newspapers, yawned and muttered, "Tomorrow. Tomorrow

I must remember to thank Martha for bringing me these papers."

Reaching out, she took the first paper that came to hand and opened it. Instantly she was wide-awake. Staring her in the face was the headline:

ROBOT IN PETRANOVA SPEAKS TO HIS

FRIENDS IN TINSALL

The headline was followed by an account of the Ponyteers' visit to Jodrell Bank. It went into great detail about their conversation with Jupiter, who announced that he was on his way back to Tinsall now that his mission to Petranova had been safely accomplished. And it also gave a full account of an interview with Uchtred, leader of the "gentle people", in which he thanked each of the Ponyteers in turn for the brave part they had played in the victorious battle that had raged under the dark side of the hill. Uchtred ended the interview by inviting them to spend a holiday in his kingdom, on the peaceful side of Petranova.

The newspaper had included a full page of photographs, which the girls shared with Alex and Ginger Tomkins, to remind readers of their past exploits. And it ended the story by saying that Jupiter and the spaceship would be arriving in Tinsall within the next few days!

This was staggering news. Sleep was forgotten. Bertha heaved herself out of bed, took one of the rickety chairs and placed it by the window. She sat down and looking out towards the high peak, tried to digest what she had read. One thing was sure, in the past, the very mention of the word Ponyteers would have sent her into a paroxysm of rage. Not any more. All the hatred stored up inside her was directed at one person, and one person only: her cousin, Mabel, the commandant.

But in order to defeat Mabel, Bertha first had to escape from Black Rock. She stared out of the window. There had to be a safe route in and out. Had to be. Then Martha's words came back to her and she sat bolt upright in her chair as she remembered them. "Ten o'clock at night. Look out to the high peak…. He always comes from that direction… Megan didn't get back 'til five in the morning…"

Bertha was ecstatic; she'd cracked it, found the way out. So simple, why hadn't she thought of it before? But hang on a minute. Maybe it was all too simple. Bertha remembered the grim fate of Mrs Blackstone and Mrs Johnson. They thought they had found a way out too – and what happened to them? Bertha was cautious. She didn't rush into things. She worked out a plan to test her theory. She liked it, because if the plan failed she wouldn't be the one to get hurt. Oh dear, no. It would be someone else – Red One!

Mrs Eastly went into her wardrobe and began rummaging about until she found what she was looking for – the WMP that Red One had smuggled into her cloak. She pressed a button, Red One answered and they had a long chat.

Martha came to her room the next night for their usual gossip. She was terribly excited and couldn't wait to tell Bertha the news. "Next week," she said breathlessly, "Next week, she's going to Cader Idris for three whole days. Three whole days, mark you."

"What's going on?" Bertha asked. She was very interested. Very interested indeed. She had a feeling that this was it. This was the opportunity she had been waiting for – the opportunity to escape.

"It's Megan's brother, David," Martha said. "He's getting engaged to a German princess. Oh, it'll be a grand affair, so it will. Magicians, sorcerers, important people from all over the world, they'll all be there at Cader Idris, to celebrate the occasion."

Mrs Eastly put on an act, pretending that the news about David's engagement to the German princess was terribly exciting. In truth, she couldn't have cared less about it.

But when their evening chat had ended and Martha had departed, Bertha could hardly contain herself, her excitement was no longer an act – it was real and she called out in a loud voice, "Just one more week! Just one more week, and its cheerio and goodbye to this place forever! And as for you, dear Mabel, just one more week and then watch out – your days as commandant are numbered!"

Bertha was smiling in her sleep; she was having a most wonderful dream. She was dreaming that her cousin Mabel had been defeated in battle and was serving a life sentence on Black Rock!

Oh yes, if dreams were anything to go by, things were looking up for Bertha, but on the other hand, they were looking distinctly *bleak* for her cousin, Mabel, the commandant.

CHAPTER EIGHT

MONSTERS FROM THE DEEP!

In the village of Tinsall the Ponyteers were talking about the proposed trip to Petranova. Surprisingly, their parents had agreed it was okay to go. Leanne was now in favour of the trip and Laura was most definitely in favour. But there was a certain amount of ambivalence on the part of Alison and Lindsey; seemingly, they could not, or would not, make up their minds about it. A short while ago they were keen to go and now they couldn't decide one way or the other. Laura and Leanne couldn't understand it; they felt that Alison and Lindsey were holding something back and it left them feeling hurt and frustrated. But their feeling of frustration wasn't to be long lived; happily everything was resolved on a day out in Chester when something rather special happened.

The bus to Chester was almost empty when it arrived at the village stop. Three boys sat on some seats near the front. There were no other passengers. The Ponyteers ignored the boys; they walked past them and sat down in some seats at the back of the bus. They were going to Chester to help

Laura spend her birthday money, a gift from Professor Klopstock. "He's lovely – and generous," Laura said. "There's enough here for new jeans and a new top."

"More than that, Laura," they chorused. And they were right. Laura had told them how much money she had received from the professor. After buying the jeans, they'd worked out that Laura would have enough money left over to buy at least a dozen new tops, providing that was what she wanted, of course.

"Well, it sure is going to be fun finding out," said Laura.

The boys at the front of the bus had started to lark about and show off.

"Ignore them," said Lindsey, applying her lipstick. "They're only doing it to attract our attention."

"Just a touch, that's all you need, Lindsey," Leanne cautioned her, pointing to her own lips.

Meanwhile Alison was busy with her hand mirror, comb and hairspray.

Why, mused Leanne, were Lindsey and Alison so particular about their appearance today?

After a while the boys settled down and began to talk about football and they were still talking football when at last the bus reached Chester. All the passengers alighted and went on their way.

The girls linked arms and hurried along towards the boutiques on The Rows. Laura loved the quaint black and white Tudor-styled timber buildings with steps leading up from the ground level shops to the first floor Rows. In and out of shops and up and down steps they went, sometimes stopping to listen to the buskers, especially if the busking musicians were violinists! Shopping for clothes was great fun, and they helped Laura discard and select so many different garments before she made her final choice that, in the end, they could scarcely remember what she had bought. Helping Laura and laden with parcels, Lindsey had just skipped down a flight of steps to street level when, to her amazement, she collided with Bill Eastly, and Alison, following on her heels, almost tripped over Bill's twin brother, Andy. The girls' parcels went flying from their hands and landed on the pavement. Bill and Andy picked them up and handed them to the girls, apologising profusely. Bill was the first to recognise them. In a loud voice he called out, "Hey! Andy. If it isn't the girl who called us monsters from the deep." His face was stern. Hands on hips he glared at Lindsey until she blushed. Bill laughed and she looked up. "I was only joking, Lindsey," he said. "Your name, it is Lindsey, isn't it?"

"Yes," she said, weakly. "I'm sorry I called you monsters..."

Bill interrupted. "Not your fault, Lindsey. It's Andy and I who should be apologising. Look, we were just going for a coffee. Would you two and your friends care to join us? I feel there's an awful lot to talk about."

The twins' suggestion that they should join them for coffee made Alison and Lindsey feel really grown up and they felt they must look every bit as old as the Eastly twins, who were now 18!

Conversation over coffee was slow to take off at first but it soon gathered pace and before they realized it an hour and a half had passed. It was time to catch the bus home and the Eastly twins offered to escort the girls back to the bus station.

Lindsey hung on to Bill's arm and Alison held Andy's arm, while Leanne and Laura walked on behind.

"Easy to see why they've doubts about Petranova," said Leanne.

"Yeah," said Laura. "Well, their secret's out now. They don't want to leave Bill and Andy." She sighed. "I can understand how they feel."

"Me too," said Leanne. "Mind you, the scientists at Jodrell Bank worked out that maybe we'd be back in Tinsall almost as soon as we left – that's if the speed of the new spaceship's what it's cracked up to be."

"Speed of light and all that stuff. I didn't have a clue what they were going on about," said Laura. "Drop it, Leanne. You're giving me a headache."

Leanne, who was as much in the dark as Laura, was only too pleased to drop the subject.

Later, when they were gathered at Laura's cottage, watching her parade up and down in her new clothes, quite out of the blue Lindsey said, "Would you and Leanne like to join Alison and me in a sort of… adventure?"

Laura stopped her parading. "What sort of an adventure?" she said, cagily. She was being cautious and rightly so. All their previous adventures had been fraught with danger, every single one of them. She reminded Lindsey of that and said, "I've had enough of adventures, Lindsey, thank you very much."

Alison recognised and understood Laura's feelings. She said, "It's not like you think, Laura. Andy and Bill, they've heard about a really cool engagement party that's going to take place in the sorcerer's castle on Cader Idris, in North Wales. We could go just for an afternoon. You know, hide and take a look and see what's gong on. The twins know of a secret passage, a special way we can get into the castle. When they were kids Mrs Eastly took them there, it was then that they found it. It's not dangerous. The sorcerer, David, who lives there, he's getting engaged to a German princess who's supposed to be really beautiful. And there'll be fantastic guests there, Laura. Wouldn't it be great to sit there in our secret hiding place and watch it all happen?"

"Count me in," said Leanne. She was excited, because it all sounded so romantic and exotic. "A real German princess," she said. "And beautiful, too."

Laura, who didn't want to be the odd one out, said, "It's all right you talking, but how will we get there – it's so far away?"

"The twins are going to hire a people carrier to drive there," said Lindsey. "Lots of seats. Don't worry, there'll be room for all of us, okay?"

"Okay, so when is it? When is this fab do?" asked Leanne.

Lindsey tapped her mobile. "They'll ring us," she said. "They'll give us plenty of warning."

In their excitement the Ponyteers had forgotten how difficult it would be to persuade their parents to consent to this special outing. Without mentioning their plans to anyone they waited for Andy or Bill to phone them.

CHAPTER NINE

THE SORCERER'S CASTLE
ON CADER IDRIS

The call from Bill Eastly came sooner than they expected and within a week they were all standing at the foot of Cader Idris. Their car was parked behind some rocks at the side of the narrow mountain road; it was completely hidden from the view of passing traffic.

Andy was poking around and peering through some bushes. The bushes were in very poor shape, stunted in growth they appeared to be struggling desperately for survival. Alison asked him what he was looking for.

"Steps. They should be here." Frowning, Andy continued to search, using his hands and feet. A minute later he parted the stunted-looking greenery and let out a whoop, "Found them!" He waved an arm, "Come on. Up here everybody, follow me," and off he went. They followed.

Roughly hewn out of the mountain's rock face, the steps were set at a steep angle; upwards they went, up and up, until finally they disappeared into a bank of cloud and mist that was advancing slowly but surely down the mountain slope. It was getting colder.

Leanne saw the cloud and the mist and didn't like the look of it. She was tired and gasping for breath. "It's crazy, we'll never make it through that lot. The mountain ridge is nearly 900 metres high. I looked it up. We're not mountain goats, you know," she said, complaining.

Andy said sympathetically, "We're not going to the top, Leanne. Nowhere near. See that bit sticking out?" He stopped climbing and pointed. He was pointing to a promontory that was no more than 50 metres higher up the mountain from where they were standing and it was clear of cloud.

"I see it," said Leanne. They others gathered around. Out of breath, they were glad of a rest.

"Yep. Well, take a good look, because that's where the castle is," said Andy.

Bill took over the talking. "Thing is, you can't really see the castle from here. It's the way it's sited. You'd have to be further round the slope to see everything. The original steps leading up to the castle are still there, but nowadays they are seldom used. Most visitors prefer to use the high speed lift, it takes them from the bottom of the mountain and drops them off just outside the castle gates."

Lindsey shivered; she did up the top button of her coat and said, "Draughty old broomsticks, nice warm lift? No contest!"

Bill laughed. "Now that I see that you've got your breath back, shall we press on?" And without waiting for an answer, he took the lead. Lindsey followed; she was never more than a single pace behind him. The others trailed after them.

Time passed. They were beginning to tire and run out of breath again when Bill said they could stop and take a rest. They sat on the steps to recover; he left them and went to explore an area that lay hidden behind a fall of rocks to the right. He'd only been away for a few minutes when he called to them, "Okay, Andy. Okay everybody, it's still here." Waving excitedly, he beckoned them to come over and see.

They joined him; he was standing behind one of the large rocks and looking into a small cave-like entrance that had been cut into the side of the mountain. It looked dark and forbidding. The twins had come prepared; they shone their torches and Bill went in first, to lead the way. The others followed, with Andy taking up the rear. The cave entrance led into a low narrow passage, it slanted upwards and they had to stoop to avoid banging their heads. Bill issued a warning for them to take care, warning them that it was wet and slippery underfoot. They took care and whenever they could, they felt the rough wall of the passage seeking handholds. They were searching for something to grip and hold onto whilst they trod the hazardous path that led them onwards and upwards and ever closer to the sorcerer's castle on Cader Idris.

"Not far now," Bill called. "Two or three minutes and we'll be there."

He wasn't far out with his timing. Rounding a bend in the tunnel, the passage suddenly widened. It was higher and it was lit almost as bright as day. Bill and Andy put away their torches; they were no longer needed. The light came streaming in through the many small square window-shaped holes in the high wall that now stood as an obstacle before them. The wall stretched upwards from the floor they stood on and ended at the roof, high above their heads. They could go no further. Beyond that wall lay the sorcerer's castle.

Andy pointed to the holes in the wall. "The holes and the tunnel, years ago they were part of the castle's ventilation system. Not now. They're not needed. Nowadays, the whole of the castle is air-conditioned."

He stopped talking and took a look through one of the windows. Light wasn't the only thing streaming in from them; there was the sound of music and the sound of human voices – happy voices. "Take a peek," said Andy. "Take a peek and you'll see what's going on."

"Well, that's what we came for," said Laura, happily. She positioned herself and peered through one of the windows. The others followed her example and marvelled at what they saw.

The room below was vast. Massive gold pillars and arches seemed to go soaring up and up forever to support the high ceiling. As the sun came out, its rays penetrated the glassed dome that occupied the central position in the ceiling and, reflected by the gilded pillars and arches, for a few magical moments, the room was bathed in a rich golden glow. The girls were overcome with awe.

Andy said, "It's the main banqueting hall, concert hall, reception hall…"

He hadn't quite finished what he was about to tell them when he was interrupted by Alison. "Reminds me of the Alhambra, Granada in Spain, remember we went there on a school visit?" She was talking to Leanne, Lindsey and Laura. They were nodding their heads excitedly and saying, "You're right, Alison, you're right."

Andy made another attempt to finish what he had set out to say. "But there are differences, Alison," he said. He pointed a finger at something that was almost hidden away in a far corner of the room and he proclaimed dramatically, "Behold the Court of the Lions. That white alabaster basin that you see before you is supported by 12 white marble lions…"

He didn't get any further, this time it was Laura who interrupted him, "Who do you think you're kidding, Andy? They're not white lions supporting that basin, no way! And whatever creatures they're supposed to be, well, take another look. They're not even white…"

"I was just about to explain," said Andy, patiently. "David likes Spain and the Alhambra, but he loves Wales. So, out went the white marble lions and in came the dragons. They're Welsh dragons supporting the basin, Laura, red dragons! It's David's choice. I admire him for it."

There was little point in trying to say more. Andy didn't want to shout, the dance music coming up from below was very loud and his throat was dry. He didn't feel like competing. He decided to stay quiet and give his throat a rest.

The music played on and beautiful women, elegant in their brilliantly coloured, beaded and embroidered gowns, swept around the room unaware that six pairs of eyes were on them.

"Just see those dresses," said Leanne, enviously

"And just dig those colours," Alison said, imitating Laura's American accent perfectly. "Those saris – out of this world."

Lindsey saw a beautiful Chinese girl wearing a cheongsam. High collared, tight fitting and daringly cut with slits up the sides. Lindsey thought it was the most exciting dress she had seen in her life. She could hardly stop talking about it.

Leanne and Laura watched the dancers swirling around the ballroom wearing the most exquisite gowns they had ever seen. Leanne said, "Do you think we'll ever be able to afford one of those, Laura?"

"You bet," said Laura. "When we discover our next treasure hoard, we'll buy one for every day in the week." Laura exuded self-confidence. Always positive in her outlook, Leanne thought the girl from San Francisco was a real treasure – the best.

The band stopped playing and the dancers retired to their tables. An announcement was made. There would be a short interval and during that time, some world famous magicians would entertain them. By popular request David's father was asked to be the first to perform. He appeared in a puff of smoke, seemingly from out of nowhere, and the crowd applauded. He stooped a little; otherwise he would have been as tall as his son, David. His hair was long and white and it grew down past his shoulders. His eyes were as black as Welsh anthracite. He had a long white beard and a moustache that grew into it.

He said his performance would be brief. Out of his magician's gown he produced his magic wand and pointed it at the 12 Welsh dragons that were supporting the white alabaster basin. Instantly, they were alive! Roaring, belching smoke and flame, they began to stamp their feet and unfurl their wings. The guests began to shriek with panic, many of them began to flee the room.

David's father waved his wand again. Instantly everything became still and calm.

"Told you my performance would be brief," he said, and he laughed. His laugh echoed round the room and it stayed long after he'd gone to wherever he went, when he'd disappeared in a quick black puff of smoke.

The applause was tumultuous and the frightened guests who had left the room crept shamefacedly back to their tables.

A second magician took the floor. He was carrying a box in each hand and he set them down on the floor. He looked nervous and at the end of his brief introduction, said, "So, it's a gentle bit of magic for you this time, to counter the drama of the last. I call it 'the ballet of the doves'. I hope you like it." And he bowed to the audience.

The orchestra began to play soft gentle music and the magician bent down and lifted the lid from one of his boxes. Too late, he realized his mistake. His face paled. Horror-stricken, he leapt back, keeping well clear of the ugly bird-like creatures with the long trailing hair that came pouring out of the box. "It's the wrong box, David. I've opened the wrong box! And their hair, David, their hair, it's deadly. I don't know what to do. Help me, David. Help me, I don't know what to do." The poor man looked terrified.

The crowd loved it. They thought it was all part of the act and they cheered and applauded.

But it wasn't part of the act. The magician had made a mistake, and it was a deadly serious mistake. The bird-like creatures that were pouring out of the box were evil spirits and one touch from a strand of their long hair could spell disaster. Even now, they were seeking high places in the roof so they could swoop down and launch an attack on the unsuspecting crowd below.

David saw the danger and acted immediately. A reassuring word to his German bride to be and he was standing by the unfortunate magician. To the "oohs" and "aahs" of the audience an amazing thing happened – David was growing in stature. He grew and grew, until he appeared to be at least three times his normal height. Then, with outstretched arms and in a voice that boomed like thunder, he issued his command:

Evil spirits return at once from whence ye came
Or be consumed in a Welsh dragon's flame.

It was no idle threat. He pointed with his wand and 12 Welsh dragons began to stamp their feet, and with a thunderous roar they belched smoke and flame high up to the roof. The castle shook. The mountain on which the castle was built seemed to shake. Singed by the heat from the dragons' fiery breath the evil spirits screamed in terror and scrambled, fighting one another, to be the first to get back into the box. The magician muttered his thanks to David and closed the lid.

The audience loved it. Ballet of the doves. They thought it had been a joke, a send up, and they clapped and they cheered for a very long time. They never did get to know the truth. David, now back to his normal size, patted the magician on the back and congratulated him on a very fine show. The man bowed and crept away with his two boxes and thanked his lucky stars that the show was over…

But the show wasn't over. Not yet. Three of the poisonous little beasts had got themselves trapped trying to escape through the holes in the wall. Now they were struggling frantically to free themselves and launch an attack on Bill, Andy and the girls. They had to get away from the sorcerer, the castle and the dragons. This was their only way out.

"Get out. Leanne, Lindsey, Laura, Alison, get back to the car," Bill yelled. He looked scared.

"What'll they do if they get through? Can't kill us, can they?" Leanne asked, striving to stay calm.

"Worse," said Andy. "It's their hair. One touch of that and you'll become one of them!"

The girls screamed. They didn't need to be told any more, they just turned and ran.

Except for Alison. She stood her ground. Two of the deadly creatures were almost free; she could almost touch them and any second now they would be in flight. She knew that no matter how fast they ran they would be no match for the winged creatures. Andy stayed with her; he kept tugging at her arm and urging her to make a run for it. She wouldn't. Alison groped in her bag and found what she was looking for – her tin of hair spray. Holding it firmly in her hand she trained the nozzle on the beasts that were trying to squeeze out through the holes in the wall. She pressed the button hard and kept pressing it. The spray had the most devastating effect on two of the little monsters. It stuck to their eyelashes, they couldn't open their eyes and they couldn't see. In the end they gave up the struggle. Without moving, they lay where they were, trapped in the hole in the wall.

The third and last of the trio had managed to free itself; it had fallen to the ground and was testing its wings. It was all set to launch itself at Alison when she saw it and directed the spray, full force, onto its wings. The beast stayed on the ground; with its wings stuck to its body it couldn't fly. For a while it lay there, its screams becoming weaker and weaker. In the end it became silent. Not a sound came from it and it didn't move again.

"I think its dead," said Andy, probing gingerly with his foot. "I think they're all dead, Alison. It's safe now. Come, I think we should go. Let's run and try to catch up with the others."

They ran down the passage, Andy leading the way, guiding Alison with his torch. Several times she nearly slipped and fell. The last time it happened the tin of hairspray fell out of her hand. It bounced and rolled down the passage ahead of them. It caught on something and stopped rolling. "Leave it," cried Alison, "I'll buy a new one tomorrow." For some reason, her remark made Andy laugh, he thought it was funny. They didn't stop running and he didn't stop laughing until they reached the car.

Once they were safely aboard, Bill started the engine and they were on their way back to the village of Tinsall.

During the journey home they couldn't thank Alison enough for saving them from what would have been a terrible fate and they asked her how she had thought of the hair spray. She couldn't tell them. She had no answer to the question. "I don't know what made me do it," she said. "When I saw them coming at us through that hole in the wall, without even thinking, I went into my handbag. And before I knew what was happening I was spraying the stuff all over them." She was so relieved that they were now safe and on their way home, she made a little joke about it. "Those hairy monsters," she said. "They hated my hairspray even more than those boys on the bus!"

They all yelled, "Please, Alison. Don't ever think of changing it. You never know, one day we might need it again!" Little did they know how true that was to be.

The Eastly twins dropped them off in the centre of the village. As they said their goodbyes, Bill asked them what they were doing in the evening. It wasn't an invitation; it was just a polite parting question. Leanne said, "Sleepover at Alison's. Girls only, Bill."

Bill blushed.

What a nice person he is, thought Leanne. So mature. It would be lovely to have a boyfriend like him. She put the thought to one side. She had piles of homework to do and the exams were looming up. She thought of Alison's mother, who opined that girls were more mature than boys of their own age and shrugged her shoulders in doubt…

"Goodbye, Bill. Bye Andy," she said, as the twins climbed into the car.

Andy called out, "Goodbye, Leanne. Goodbye, girls. And thanks, Alison, you know…"

"Yeah, Andy, I know…" said Alison.

Andy closed the door and the car sped away.

CHAPTER TEN

ESCAPE FROM BLEAK COURT
ON BLACK ROCK

What Martha had told Mrs Eastly a week ago turned out to be true. Megan's brother, David, the sorcerer from Cader Idris, came on his white-winged horse and took Megan away with him. She would be gone for three whole days, that's what Martha said. Martha was always right about these things. She was a close confidant of Megan's and Megan told her everything.

The day after Megan had departed for Cader Idris, Mrs Eastly made up her mind that this was her only chance to be free. It was now or never. This was the day she was going to escape from Bleak Court. She opened her mobile phone to speak to Red One. They had a long serious conversation about escape plans and made the necessary arrangements.

At ten minutes to ten that night Mrs Eastly sat down on one of the rickety chairs in front of the window. She looked out; it was a cold, bright, clear night, ideal for flying. But Bertha was worried. Earlier in the day there had been a warning over the radio that later in the evening mist and fog could be expected to spread over a wide area. Mrs Eastly crossed her fingers and made a wish.

At five minutes to ten she looked at her watch. She got out of her chair and switched her room light on and then off, repeating this signal every minute as Red One had requested.

She was staring out towards the high peak and at ten o'clock precisely she saw Red One approaching from quite a long way off. Red One was flying fairly low and pretty well in line with the window. However, something was not quite right about her flight and it took Bertha a minute or two to make out what it was. The flight was erratic – up and down, side-to-side – it brought an anxious look to Bertha's face. It was a crazy performance. What was Red One playing at? Was she in control, or not? Would she make it safely to Bleak Court, or would she end up having a fatal accident like the others? It wasn't until Red One had reached the high wall that surrounded the courtyard that her flight became stable. Bertha sighed with relief. She flung open the window and in one smart manoeuvre Red One was standing beside her.

"Really, it's more like flying in a tunnel than in a corridor," explained Red One, drawing an imaginary tunnel in the air with a gloved hand.

"But you were flying so erratically. I was worried about your safety," said Mrs Eastly. Her voice sounded full of concern for the young woman who had come to rescue her. But her sympathy was false. Mrs Eastly's concern was for herself. She had no thought for Red One or anyone else.

"Worried about my safety? Oh! That's really sweet of you, Sister Bertha," said Red One, feeling genuinely touched by Mrs Eastly's concern. "Actually there was no danger. No danger at all. I was testing to see how much space was going spare in the tunnel. Not much, and that's a fact. I discovered something, though."

"What did you discover?" Bertha asked, anxiously.

"I discovered that flight outside the limits of that tunnel is impossible and it would be certain death to try," said Red One.

She spoke about it so coolly; Mrs Eastly couldn't help but admire her. But why, why was she doing all this for her? Bertha felt she had to ask the question, "Why are you helping me, Red One? I mean, well, it's so risky, to say the least. And if you ever get found out…"

"Don't you worry about that, Sister Bertha, I like taking risks."

"But why? Why take risks on my account?"

"Because I hate Red Leader. Simple as that – that's why. She's in my way. I'll never get promotion while she's around. In any case, I'm fed up with the present lot. Now, with you in command, Sister Bertha, things would be different. I reckon I could go places if you were commandant."

Mrs Eastly could not believe what she was hearing. She said emphatically, "Well, you can forget all about that, young lady. I wouldn't have the commandant's job, not if you paid me a fortune. No, my dear, the woman you want for that job is Jackie Fife. You know Jackie Fife – pots of money, lives in that large house on the river Dee?"

Red One hesitated. "Know her? Not really. Jackie Fife? I overheard the chief of security talking to the commandant about her once – she was laughing and calling her 'Jack the Knife'. I don't know why."

Mrs Eastly didn't know why Jackie had been referred to by that title either. She said to Red One, "Talking of names, it seems daft me calling you Red One, when we are so closely involved – and such *friends*."

Mrs Eastly had a great way with using words that flattered. She'd used them successfully with young Martha at Bleak Court and now she'd done it again with Red One. Red One liked it when Bertha said she was her friend. "My name's Ruth," she said. "Ruth Davenport's my name. Call me Ruth. But if you don't mind me hurrying you, Bertha, I think we should be on our way. That escape tunnel, well, we don't know for sure how long it will stay open, do we? If we miss it now we could be stuck here until five in the morning."

"You're right about that," said Bertha. "That's why poor Johnny couldn't get away. The escape path was closed."

"Johnny, who's Johnny?" Ruth asked.

"Not now. Tell you later," said Mrs Eastly. She picked up her bag. "Come on, let's go."

"By the way," said Ruth, as she prepared the broomstick for take-off. "Is there an inmate here called Fairfax? Mrs Fairfax?"

"Yes."

"Did you tell her anything about your plans to escape?

"No, I didn't. I couldn't stand the woman. Why do you ask?"

"Because she's a plant. An informer. A spy," said Ruth. "Everything, anything you said to her would be relayed to HQ."

"Well, she got nothing out of me. Nothing at all, I couldn't stand the sight of the woman," said Mrs Eastly.

Mounting the broomstick together they made a successful take-off from the window of Bertha's room in Bleak Court and they kept the high peak directly in front of them as they flew out from Black Rock. Only once did Ruth deviate from track and that was by way of demonstration. She moved slowly left, until she was on the extreme edge of the tunnel and Bertha felt the savage pull of severe turbulence on her

96

left leg. The strength of the wind hit the left side of her body and she feared that she was about to be ripped away from the broomstick. She felt for Ruth's belt and held on to it tightly. The broomstick was eased back onto a safer course and Bertha managed to stifle the scream of terror that had been trying to escape from her lips. "See what I mean, Bertha? " Ruth said, by way of explanation.

Mrs Eastly didn't say anything. She was too frightened to speak.

Once they had crossed the mainland coast and well inland they were clear of the escape tunnel and its dangers. At last they were safe!

Ruth swayed her body slightly to the left. "Next stop, Jackie Fife's place, in Chester," she said.

But she was wrong. It wasn't Ruth's fault, she seldom made mistakes, but this time she did make an error and it was all due to the weather. It had suddenly become misty, very misty indeed. Ruth was worried. They were flying low and she asked Bertha to keep an eye open for pylons, tall trees and high buildings. Bertha's eyes darted from side to side like fish in a tank. She knew she would get hurt, or worse, if they crashed. She strained her eyes looking for obstacles. The mist got thicker. It turned into dense fog until they could hardly see a yard in front of them. Bertha gave up; she closed her eyes and waited for the worst to happen. She was convinced they were about to crash.

She thought that the dreaded moment had come when the broomstick began to judder. "What's happening, Ruth?" she yelled, her eyes now open wide with terror.

Ruth's voice remained calm; she was looking down at the ground below. "It's much clearer here," she said as she picked out Red House Farm in the distance. "We've come too far, Bertha. We've overshot Chester."

The broomstick juddered violently again. Bertha said nervously, "Never mind overshooting Chester. Why's this broomstick jumping up and down all the time?"

"We've run out of time, Bertha. These broomsticks are time programmed for patrol duties. Each patrol has a set time limitation. It's like running out of petrol." Ruth's voice remained steady and calm.

"You mean, you mean we might run out of petrol – I mean time – and crash!" Bertha was almost screaming with fear.

"'Fraid so," said Ruth. The broomstick juddered again, this time more violently than ever. Bertha reached for Ruth's belt to hang on to. Low moaning sounds came from her lips.

Ruth reached for her microphone and spoke into it. Her voice was urgent. "Mayday. Mayday. Mayday. This is Red One, to Witches' Emergency Control Centre. Crash imminent! Chester area. Red One to Witches' Emergency Control Centre. Mayday, over." Ruth pressed her identification button on her microphone and left it switched on.

The duty controller at the centre identified their blip on her radar tube by the identification mark that trailed behind it. She responded immediately, "Emergency Control to Red One, you are over the village of Tinsall. Sending search and rescue team straight away, over."

There was no reply from Red One. The broomstick had struck the ground close to the giant oak tree that grew in the paddock field behind Alison's house and burst into flames. Bertha was not wearing a flying suit and if it had not been for Ruth's quick thinking she would have been badly burned. Her thick, black cloak was on fire when Ruth dragged her clear of the blazing broomstick. Ruth tore the cloak from her shoulders and stamped on it until she had

98

put out the flames. She left it lying in the damp grass. It was badly scorched and Ruth wondered if it would be fit for Bertha ever to wear again.

The time was almost midnight and in Tinsall, Lindsey, Leanne and Laura were having a sleepover at Alison's house. They were wide awake and chatting excitedly about the events of the day; their visit to the sorcerer's castle at Cader Idris, all those beautiful dresses in the ballroom, the Welsh dragons and the flying monsters with the hair that, if it touched you, could change you into one of them! And the Eastly twins – it was Bill this and Andy that for ages. They just couldn't bring themselves to say goodnight and try to go to sleep.

Lindsey had wandered over to the window and looked out. The mist had all but cleared. Her eyes picked out the large leafy tree in the middle of the paddock and it reminded her of happy days in the summer when the ponies would shelter in its shade, away from the heat of the sun. Then she saw the lights, they were bobbing up and down, flying and circling the tree, she recognised them at once – they were witches on broomsticks! She froze. Scared, she called out and the others came over to look.

Leanne put a protective arm around her sister. "They're looking for something," she said, squinting with her eyes, trying to get used to the light.

"And they've found what they're looking for," cried Laura. "Look, they're flying away on their broomsticks and there's two on one of them."

The lights and the broomsticks disappeared. "What do you make of that then?" asked Leanne. She waited, but no one could give an answer.

"Think I'll text Bill tomorrow," said Lindsey, "Tell him what's happened. See what he thinks."

"Yeah, and I'll text Andy, and ask him," said Alison.

They were so busy talking they did not see the lone figure of Mrs Eastly emerge from her hiding place in the hedgerows. Nor did they see her set off on foot for Chester. Had they done so, the girls' sleepover may well have ended in nightmare!

CHAPTER ELEVEN

THE WITCH FINDS A SAFE HAVEN

It was in the early hours of the morning, almost three o'clock, when Mrs Eastly arrived outside Jackie Fife's house on the river Dee. She rang the bell and beat on the door with her fists until somebody answered. It was Jackie herself who opened the door. "Why, if it isn't Bertha Eastly," she exclaimed. She ran her eyes over the dishevelled figure standing before her. "Oh, you poor dear. Oh, you poor, poor…" That's all Bertha heard before she collapsed in a heap at Jackie's feet.

Later that same morning, Red Three stopped Red One as she came out of the commandant's office. "What's the verdict," she asked.

"Six months' loss of seniority," came the bitter reply. "Said I was negligent. Bang goes my chance of promotion now."

Red Three said she was sorry. But Red One knew that she wasn't. With Red One off the promotional ladder, her job would be up for grabs and that look in Red Three's eyes said it all – she wanted that job for herself.

101

Red One had the last word. "I'm not worried. You know what they say, 'When one door closes, another one opens.'" She wore an odd little smile on her face when she said it. It didn't go unobserved by Red Three. She apologised, said she was busy, had things to do and couldn't stop to talk. But as she walked away she speculated that Red One was up to something. It was Red One's odd little smile that gave the game away and her remark, "When one door closes another one opens," that was so suspicious. Oh yes, Red Three knew that Red One was up to something, but for the life of her she could not figure out what it was.

In Tinsall, the girls woke up in the morning and decided to go and search for clues – anything that might tell them something about the strange events they had witnessed the night before. It didn't take long before they discovered the charred remains of Red One's broomstick.

"I think we should report this to Juno," said Leanne. "See what she thinks."

They agreed and all set off to tell the robot what they had discovered.

As they arrived at her workshop they heard the sound of music through the open door. It had a great beat to it and they stopped and listened for a while before going into the workshop. As soon as she saw them Juno stopped playing.

"No, no, Juno, don't stop playing, it's great!" exclaimed Alison.

"More, more," urged Lindsey, enthusiastically.

Juno nodded. "Thanks, Lindsey," she said. "Jupiter thinks my playing is real cool. Do you think its cool?" She didn't wait for a reply. Instead, she gave them another short recital, which she ended with a flourish of her metal hands. Then she spoke to them in her funny chopped-up voice, "I can s-ee by the l-ook on your faces that you didn't c-ome to hear mu-sic. You're wor-ried, I c-an tell. Come on, girls, out with it."

They didn't hesitate. They were bursting to tell her what they had witnessed the previous night. "The broomstick must have caught fire," said Alison. "And we found a black burnt-out patch in the middle of the paddock."

"And some burnt-out bits of a broomstick," added Laura.

"Well, if you're worried because you think that Mrs Eastly might be involved, forget it," said Juno. "She's l-ocked up in a prison. About two weeks ago I saw security officers arrest her and take her off to a place called B-leak Court on B-lack Rock. No one ever escapes from that place, and that's a fact." She didn't tell the girls about Alex and Ginger being changed into mice. She didn't want to frighten them.

Reassured, the girls went away to groom and feed their ponies, but before closing the door behind them, Lindsey stopped to say, "Jupiter's not the only one who thinks you're cool, Juno. We all do. In fact, I think you're very cool."

Juno placed her metallic fingers to her lips and the sound of a happy little giggle filtered through them.

It was almost four o'clock in the morning before Mrs Eastly had recovered sufficiently to be put to bed. Two cups of steaming hot cocoa, each with three spoonfuls of sugar, had helped to revive her. Then, with Jackie's support, Bertha found her way up the winding staircase and she lay on the bed, while Jackie relieved her of her muddy boots and scorched cloak. She fell asleep still wearing all her other clothes and Jackie threw a blanket over her to keep

103

her warm before creeping out of the room. Bertha did not wake up until five o'clock in the evening.

By eight o'clock that night, Bertha was feeling much better. She'd had a nice hot bath and a change of clothes. True, the clothes were a bit tight here and there; after all they belonged to Jackie. But at least they were clean, clean and warm.

Bertha and Jackie were sitting down having their evening meal together, when Jackie asked, "Well, Bertha, what's all the news from Bleak Court?"

Mrs Eastly told her about Mrs Blackstone, who had used her magic to turn herself into a fish so that she could swim to safety, only to be gobbled up by an even bigger fish the moment she had struck the water. Jackie Fife was astonished. She did not say a word, she just opened and closed her mouth and looked like a fish out of water!

Bertha then described Mrs Johnson's failed attempt to escape on the stolen broomstick. She told Jackie how gale force winds had driven her back to Bleak Court no matter which way she tried to escape. And the broomstick – how finally, it had gone berserk. "It unseated poor Johnnie, sent her crashing down on the hard cobblestones below, where she had died instantly."

Bertha's stories about the two failed escapes upset Jackie. Her face was pale, but driven on by curiosity she wanted to know more.

"But you managed it, Bertha. You escaped. You found a way out. You're famous, do you know that? You are the very first person to escape from Black Rock. How did you do it?"

"Good luck, mostly," said Bertha, modestly. Then she found herself blushing with pleasure; after all it must be some sort of honour to be the first one to escape from the notorious prison on Black Rock.

Jackie Fife was not going to allow her to get away with it as easily as that. "Now, come on, Bertha. It took more than good luck. Admit it. It took a bit of that old Eastly cunning and magic. I'm right, aren't I? I can feel it in my bones."

"Well," said Bertha. Then she went on to tell Jackie about Megan, the governor of Bleak Court, and her brother, the sorcerer, from Cader Idris. "He was seated on the back of a great white-winged horse," said Bertha. "For all the world, he looked like a prince with that fine rich cloak flowing behind him."

"I know, I know, I've seen him," Jackie said excitedly, the sad look disappearing from her face. "Like you say, he's very handsome."

"It was something that Martha the maid mentioned that put me onto it," said Bertha. "She told me to watch out for him approaching with the high peak of Cader Idris behind him. Ten o'clock he would arrive. Ten o'clock at night, to take his sister, Megan, to a party. And later when she told me that Megan didn't arrive back until five the next morning, the penny dropped. I guessed that the escape route was in a direct line from the high peak of Cader Idris and Black Rock and that it was open at ten o'clock at night and five o'clock in the morning. Seems I got something right for a change."

"Got something right for a change? I think you were brilliant to work that out, Bertha, absolutely brilliant!"

Bertha found herself blushing again.

They had finished eating and were at the coffee stage. "Black or white? I've forgotten," Jackie said. She was poised with a silver coffee pot in her hand. "Worth £2,000, this little beauty," she said.

"Black," said Mrs Eastly. "Three sugars, and don't say it's bad for my weight." She ignored Jackie's remark about

105

the cost of the coffee pot. Everybody knew Jackie was rich and that she loved expensive luxuries. Bertha didn't want to talk about that. She had more important things to discuss.

Jackie seemed to have read her mind. She stopped talking about money and went back to the original subject. She poured Bertha the coffee. "Okay," she said, "so you found the escape corridor. But somebody had to fly you out. You didn't have a broomstick, so who was it who flew you out?"

Mrs Eastly swore Jackie to secrecy before telling her about Red One. Then she told her how brave Red One had been, how she had saved her life when they'd crashed. "She hates that lot, Jackie. The commandant – everybody! She could be very useful to us, Jackie, a spy in the enemy camp," she said.

Jackie agreed, but added a word of caution. "The commandant's no fool, Bertha. I think that she'll put two and two together, the crash and your escape. I think Red One might have got away with it if it hadn't been for the crash. She shrugged her shoulders. "Now, as I said, Mabel's no fool." She looked at her watch. "Have an early night, Bertha. Get some rest. Tomorrow we can talk again, okay?"

"Okay," said Bertha, satisfied that she had another willing accomplice.

CHAPTER TWELVE

THE COMMANDANT INVESTIGATES

Maureen Summers, the adjutant, was in her office. She was standing at the filing cabinet and putting away some papers relating to the trial of Red One when the phone rang. Two strides and she was sitting at her desk. She picked up the phone and listened. Whatever it was, the news must have been bad, because when the call ended Maureen looked troubled and anxious. She placed her elbows on the desk, resting her head in her hands to try and regain her composure. Two minutes resting like that and she felt better. She stood up, took a deep breath, left her office and went to see the commandant.

Maureen faced the commandant across her desk. She said, "Sorry, Ma'am, but I'm the bearer of bad news. It's very bad news, and I'm sorry, really sorry."

The commandant saw the strain on her adjutant's face and replied kindly, "Don't worry, Maureen, whatever it is, tell me. I can cope." And she nodded her head encouragingly.

The adjutant's face remained glum. The commandant smiled, "Don't hold anything back, Maureen. I promise not to shoot the messenger."

The commandant's attempt at humour was lost on Maureen. She replied, "It's your cousin, Mrs Eastly, Ma'am." She paused for a second and then the rest of what she had to say came out in a rush. "She's escaped from Black Rock, Ma'am. She's escaped! That's what I've come to tell you."

"Bertha escaped? Impossible!" The commandant leapt out of her chair and began to pace the room. She could take bad news all right – it came with the job. But Bertha's escape was something for which she was totally unprepared and it took time for the shock to wear off.

Again the adjutant spoke. "I'm sorry, but it's true, Ma'am. I've been talking to the governor, Megan. I've just put the phone down."

Composure regained, the commandant sat down again. "Megan, you spoke to her? I thought she was at Cader Idris, at her brother's engagement party?"

"Yes, she was. It was Mrs Fairfax who reported that Mrs Eastly was missing. As soon as Megan was informed, she returned to Black Rock."

Still sitting in her chair, the commandant began to scribble on the notepad in front of her. Then, speaking her thoughts out aloud, she said, "Bertha couldn't have escaped by boat. Ships and boats are definitely out. There's only one boat at Black Rock, the supply boat, and it's permanently guarded. As for escape by air, that's impossible. Megan, her brother and I are the only ones who know the secret of the escape route."

Maureen said, "But somehow she managed it. She isn't on Black Rock now, is she? We have to face up to it, Ma'am, your cousin, Mrs Eastly, has escaped!"

"Please don't give me that 'we have to face up to it routine' Maureen," said the commandant, with irritation in her voice. "I *am* facing up to it. All I'm saying is that she couldn't have accomplished the escape by herself. She couldn't have. Impossible. No, she must have had someone to help her. She had to have an accomplice. Now, I wonder who that could be?" The commandant sounded puzzled and vexed.

"Difficult to answer that one," said the adjutant. "Mrs Eastly, she wasn't the easiest of people to get on with. I can't think of a single person on whom she could count as a friend. You know, a real friend."

"Neither do I," added the commandant grimly. "But somebody helped her, that's for sure, and whoever it was, they must have talked to one another. Tell me, Maureen, my cousin, Bertha. She couldn't have had a WMP in her possession when they escorted her to Black Rock, could she?"

The adjutant hung her head. "She may have, Ma'am."

"How do you mean 'she may have, Ma'am'?" Mabel couldn't prevent the little outburst of sarcasm as she mimicked her adjutant.

Maureen winced. "Seems no one searched her clothing, here or at Black Rock. You know what they say – nobody escapes from Black Rock – they thought searching was unnecessary."

"Unnecessary!" The commandant came down heavily on the word. "Such slackness. I want the names of those who escorted my cousin to Black Rock and I've no doubt Megan will be doing the same at her end. That list, Maureen, I mean it and I want it. Is that clear?"

"Yes, Ma'am."

Calm again, the commandant felt sorry for making her adjutant look so miserable. She said, "Sorry if I came down on you a bit heavily just now, Maureen. I'm not blaming you, okay?"

Maureen looked relieved. She brightened up. "That's alright, Ma'am. And I do understand how awful all this is for you. Is there anything I can do?"

"Yes, Maureen, there is. Leave me now and ask Betty Bright, chief of intelligence, to report to me, immediately."

"Yes, Ma'am," replied the adjutant, and she scurried away to carry out the commandant's instructions.

The chief of intelligence and the commandant were locked in conversation for almost an hour. It was Betty Bright who brought the conversation to a close.

"Right," she said. "I'll take myself off to Black Rock and do a bit of digging there. Won't take long. When I come back I'll have a few questions to ask at HQ."

"At HQ. What sort of questions?"

"Oh, only what you would expect, Ma'am. For instance, on the night your cousin escaped I shall need to know the names of those who were airborne, times of landing etc etc, and I'll need to talk to them, later. To save time, perhaps you would obtain that information for me whilst I'm away?"

"Of course I will, but surely you don't suspect anyone at HQ, do you?"

"I certainly do," said the chief of intelligence, and speaking with great emphasis added, "In my opinion the accomplice is more likely to have come from here than anywhere else. With your permission, Ma'am, I need to have all HQ WMPs in my possession – now – today! I'll inspect them on my way to Black Rock. Somebody talked to your cousin, had to – to plan the escape. The answer is on one of those WMPs, I'll wager my life on it." She held out her hand, "I might as well collect yours now, Ma'am, if that's okay?"

"That's okay, Betty," said the commandant, handing over her mobile phone without protest.

"Sorry about that, Ma'am," said Betty Bright, pocketing the WMP, "but I can't leave anybody out. You do understand?"

"Perfectly," said the commandant. "I would have doubted your efficiency if you hadn't asked me for it."

"Thanks. Oh, and one last thing," said Betty. "It would save time if you checked around, see if there's anybody you know who might be hiding your cousin. Will you do that?"

"Will do," said the commandant.

"Good. Then the sooner I start the sooner I get finished. As for the name of the accomplice, you'll have that within three days, Ma'am, I promise."

"I'll keep you to that," said the commandant.

They shook hands and as she departed, the chief of intelligence said, "I meant what I said, you'll have the name of the accomplice within three days. Promise."

The commandant knew that she could rely on Betty Bright, who was as bright as her name suggested.

When the chief of intelligence left for Black Rock, the commandant called for her adjutant and spoke to her again. "Did you get it?" she asked.

"Yes, Ma'am." She handed the commandant a piece of paper. "Everything you called for is on that list: names, airborne times, etc, everything. The lot!"

The commandant ran her eye down the list and she stopped when she came to the name of Red One. "Isn't she the one we had up on a charge?"

"Yes, Ma'am. She was out on patrol that night and she crashed. Negligence. You sentenced her to six months' loss of seniority."

"Right, I remember." The commandant ran a hand through her hair. She said, "The WECC, were they involved?"

111

"Yes, Ma'am. They responded to her mayday call. They sent out a rescue party. It was about midnight when it happened. I can get exact times from the Witches' Emergency Control Centre if you wish."

"No, Maureen, that won't be necessary. The crash and the mayday call, it all fits in perfectly. I think I know who it was who helped cousin Bertha, but for the life of me, I can't understand why."

"Surely you don't suspect Red One, Ma'am?" said the adjutant.

"Yes, Maureen, I do," said the commandant. "Keep it under your hat, though, at least until I've discussed my suspicions with the chief of intelligence when she returns from Black Rock. Only then will we decide on what action to take. In the meantime I want someone to keep an eye on Red One. Will you arrange that?"

"Yes, Ma'am," said the adjutant.

"Then do it now," said the commandant.

Maureen paused at the door as she left the commandant's office and said, "Red One, she's one of the most important and skilled members of the team. You know what they say, Ma'am, and I've heard it several times. They say that she's even better than Red Leader."

"Perhaps you've hit the nail on the head there, Maureen," replied the commandant. "Maybe she thought she was better than Red Leader, too. Perhaps jealousy had a part to play in all of this?"

And the commandant, of course, was right about that.

Sitting at her desk the adjutant summoned Red Three, Sarah Leakey, to her office, and the first thing she did was to swear her to secrecy. That done, she talked about Red One and explained to Sarah the role she wanted her to play. When she had finished speaking, Red Three could hardly contain herself, "I knew she was up to something," she said, "I knew it! I knew it!"

The adjutant said, "Keep a close eye on her. Any suspicious move, especially if you think she's about to make a run for it – report it to me immediately. Understood?"

" 'Course I will, Adj. You can rely on me," said Red Three. Her eyes shone greedily. "Promise you'll put a good word in for me after – you know – about my position in the team. Yes?"

"Yes, I promise," said the adjutant. "But remember, it will be Red Leader and finally the commandant who will have last word on the subject, okay?"

"Okay, Adj."

"Off you go then, Red Three. The job starts now and don't forget, play it cool, be discrete, don't let her know you have her under observation."

Red Three laughed. "She won't know I'm watching. They didn't call me 'Sneaky Leakey' at school for nothing, you know."

"No, I don't suppose they did," said the adjutant under her breath as the door closed behind Red Three.

Sneaky Leakey was good at her job. Moving like a shadow, she flitted around the corridors and offices of HQ, never losing sight of Red One, noting every move she made. But everyone makes mistakes and Sarah Leakey was no exception. When Red One saw Sarah dodge back behind a corner she realized what was happening. They were following her! How long would it be before security officers came along to arrest her for helping in the escape of Mrs Eastly? Red One knew it was time for her to leave. No wasting time hanging about and waiting for the worst to happen. It was time to do a runner. But first she had to get rid of Sarah Leakey, otherwise the game would really be up. She didn't panic. She set her mind to work and came up with a plan. It was a good plan, it would get rid of little Miss Sneaky and also allow ample time for her own getaway.

Before entering her room, Red One made sure that Sarah Leakey was following her. Satisfied, she closed the door behind her. Quickly, she pulled a jogging outfit over the top of her flying suit and laced up a pair of trainers. Next, she removed her broomstick from its special case, dismantled it and placed it in a canvas bag together with her helmet and a few other bits and pieces of equipment. She pushed it under the bed. She was smiling. She wagged a finger and said, "Now, stay there 'til I get back."

She stepped outside her door and there was Red Three.

"Going for a run?" Sarah Leakey said to Red One, with a slightly anxious look on her face.

"No. Just a ten-minute workout in the gym, might do a couple of circuits of the hockey field after, that's if I feel up to it. Look, why don't you join me, Sarah? Exercise will do you good."

Red Three was all for it. A nice spot of exercise whilst keeping Red One under close observation, nothing would suit her better. "Love to," she said. "Wait in my room 'til I change and we'll be off. Oh, and thanks for thinking about me, Ruth."

"Don't mention it," said Red One.

Red One took the key to the equipment room off the hook and opened the door. "What are you going to get?" Red Three asked, stepping inside the room and expecting Red One to join her. Red One didn't join her. She slammed the door to the equipment room shut, locked it and called out, "Now, let's see you try to sneak out of this one, Sarah." A muffled cry came from within. Red One smiled, she pocketed the key, returned to her room and collected the canvas bag from under the bed. Then, acting swiftly, she attended to one or two other very important tasks before leaving the building. Twenty minutes later she was on a bus to Chester and heading for Jackie Fife's house that stood high up on the banks of the river Dee.

The chief of intelligence returned from Black Rock early. They were in the commandant's office. In discussing Mrs Eastly's escape, Betty Bright absolved the governor and the maid at Bleak Court from blame, saying that Bertha must have discovered the escape route by observation and pure chance. As for Mrs Fairfax, she was most scathing about her. She said she was a complete waste of time and money and in her report she would recommend her removal.

That said, the chief of intelligence emptied the contents of a large black plastic bag on the commandant's desk. They were all the witches' mobile phones. She selected one, held it up high, and said, "All the proof we need is in this little joker." Then in dramatic tones, she declared, "It's Red One! She's the accomplice! She's the one we want!" Before there was time for anyone to react to the news, the adjutant burst into the room and announced in a loud voice that Red One had disappeared. "Vanished into thin air! Within the last hour! Locked Red Three in the sports equipment room and escaped!" The commandant seemed to be stunned by the news, but not Betty Bright, she was jubilant. "Great," she said. "That's just great. Couldn't be better."

"Great! How can it be just great?" muttered the commandant, deeply puzzled.

"It means just that," said Betty. "And by this evening I shall be able to give you a full account of our enemies' plans. Thanks to Red One and her escape."

"But how can you do that if she's not here to tell us?" said the commandant. The puzzled look was still on her face.

"Red One doesn't know it, but her escape is the key to our success and the opposition's failure – trust me, Ma'am."

"Of course I trust you, Betty."

"A word of warning then, Ma'am. I have no doubt whatsoever that your cousin, Bertha, and Red One will be planning to attack us – and soon! They'll want to catch us off guard. Fortunately, by this evening, I shall know their plans. But in the meantime, and from this very moment, we are under threat. Your cousin is a dangerous woman, Ma'am, and with your permission I would like to put HQ on immediate 'Yellow Alert'."

The commandant did not hesitate. "Do it," she said, decisively.

The chief of intelligence spoke on her WMP. Within seconds, noisy hooters were blasting out warning signals and electric signs were flashing out the message "Yellow Alert! Yellow Alert!"

Meanwhile, interesting things had been happening in Tinsall. Professor Klopstock and his nephew, Eliot, had arrived from San Francisco accompanied by their friend, Bill Ferguson, an American air force general. The general was representing the president of the United States of America, who had given special permission for the American robot, Jupiter, to fly the "gentle people" back to Petranova. With that mission accomplished they were now waiting to greet Jupiter on his return flight to Tinsall and planet earth…

Lindsey and Alison had other important things to think about. They had not seen Bill and Andy since the excursion to Cader Idris, and now they had new boyfriends. In fact their new boyfriends were two of the boys who had been playing about on the bus on the day they had travelled to Chester to spend some of Laura's birthday money. Lindsey and Alison were together now and Lindsey was talking to her sister about the boys. "When you get to know them, Leanne, you'll really like them. They're not the least bit like they were on the bus; they're really quite grown up. They don't act like kids, you know."

"But they are lots of fun and good looking," added Alison, nodding her head vigorously.

"So what's the problem?" asked Leanne.

"It's Bill and Andy," said Alison. "We like them and want to be their friends, but not to go out with, you know… You must have noticed, Leanne, they are a bit old, and a bit fuddy-duddy."

"And not a bit like John Williams and Peter Snowdon," said Lindsey. "Now, they can be really funny, make you laugh."

"Well, I'm sure Bill and Andy won't mind," said Leanne. "You can remain friends with them and still have fun with boys of the same year at school. I'll speak to Bill and Andy if you like."

"Oh, will you, Leanne? Thanks, thanks a lot," chorused Lindsey and Alison, showing great signs of relief.

And when they gave Bill and Andy's mobile numbers to Leanne, they didn't notice how pleased she looked.

CHAPTER THIRTEEN

COUNCIL OF WAR

There were 13 witches in Jackie Fife's large drawing room, 14 including Red One. They were sitting in rows facing her. Behind them was a large picture window and through it Ruth could see the Roman amphitheatre and behind that a portion of the red sandstone defence walls that ringed Chester. It was early evening and the sun shone down on the sandstone casting a pink glow over the city. As she lowered her eyes, Ruth could see pleasure boats plying the river Dee and sounds of laughter and singing came through the open window.

She looked around the drawing room noting the grim faces of those in front of her. What a contrast. Not a smile to be seen. The witches were of the Old Order and friends of Mrs Eastly.

Bertha Eastly was sitting on the front row next to Jackie Fife and for the first time Ruth noticed Bertha's hands, they were resting on her knees. Ruth's eyes focussed on them. How odd, she thought, that one so fleshy could have such skeletal-like hands.

Jackie Fife made a signal for Ruth to make a start. Ruth stood up and called out in a loud voice, "Sisters, we are at war!" This dramatic statement sent a buzz of excitement around the room. Ruth paused, raised her arms and the room instantly became silent. They wanted to hear what she had to say next. She continued. "Yes, Sisters, we are at war. The decision has been taken for us. Even now, officers of the New Order are out there searching for Sister Bertha, her supporters and me." Ruth raised her voice to a louder pitch. "We must strike and defeat them before they hunt us down one by one and cage us like wild animals." Ruth's listeners began to applaud their approval; some pounded the wooden floor with their broomstick handles. Jackie Fife didn't like that. She didn't like it at all and she asked them not to do it, saying it could damage the floor, reminding them that repairs – any kind of repairs – would cost her money! Her reproof seemed to go over their heads.

Totally ignoring her, one of witches stood up, shook a fist and called out to Ruth, "We're with you all the way, Sister, tell us what we have to do and we'll do it." The witch sat down and again began to pound out her approval on Jackie's wooden floor. The others quickly followed suit. Jackie called out, pleading with them to stop damaging her floor, but they took no heed of her pleas, they just kept on pounding the floor with their broomsticks.

At last the noise died down and Ruth was able to continue. She said, "I've been asked what we should do. Well, I'll tell you what we *have* to do. We must strike tonight and attack the commandant in her lair. Tonight it must be, tomorrow is too late. And we are fortunate, for it has just been announced that the spaceship from Petranova will be landing tonight." Ruth paused to allow the buzz of excitement to die down and then she continued. "The eyes of the world will be on the village of Tinsall, so the element of surprise will be ours. Sisters, we must seize this opportunity, it may never come our way again." Again she paused and told them to listen very carefully to what she now had to say. When she was sure she had their full attention she went on. "Before escaping I planted timed explosives to the door at the rear of HQ. They are due to explode at midnight and that is the signal for our attack. At midnight tonight, we shall storm our way through the open doors of the commandant's headquarters and battle our way to victory. By the break of dawn tomorrow the headquarters building will be ours and the Old Order restored." Ruth sat down to the pounding broomstick beat on Jackie's floor and the chant, "War! War! Victory! Victory!"

Jackie didn't say a word in protest. She knew it was hopeless to try and calm them.

Gradually the chanting died down and Ruth asked the witches of the Old Order to check their watches. It was 18.30 hours precisely. Watches were checked and adjusted. "Take-off time will be 23.00 hours," Ruth announced. "We will stand off our target until we hear the sound of the explosives, then we move in. I will lead the first wave, which will include Sisters Thea and Phoebe." There was an outburst of excitement at the announcement of their names, for it was well known that their powerful magic had been handed down to them from the dawn of the universe, long before history began. "Sisters Thea and Phoebe will unleash their most deadly demons and they will devour those weaklings cowering behind the walls of the headquarters building. The second wave will carry out the mopping up operation. The final wave, including Sisters Bertha and Jackie, will secure the control room. By this time the battle will have been won, victory will be ours and the Old Order restored!"

Ruth had done with talking. She had outlined her plan for victory and the witches were with her, 100 per cent. As she sat down to a tremendous burst of cheering there was much stamping of feet and banging of broomsticks on Jackie's precious wooden floor. Jackie refrained from protesting. What was the use? Instead, she led them to a spacious dining room where a splendid cold buffet was laid out for them.

"Eat your fill," exhorted Jackie. "Eat as much as you can, for there will be no more victuals until we celebrate victory in the early hours of the morning."

The witches needed no second telling. Vast quantities of salmon, ham and meat pies disappeared – as if by magic!

Towards the end of the meal, Jackie excused herself and went upstairs to collect her handbag. Downstairs, her guests continued to gorge food and talk about the impending battle. Suddenly they heard the most awful clattering noise coming from the direction of the hall. Rushing out of the dining room they found poor Jackie lying in a heap at the foot of the stairs. She managed to whisper weakly that she believed that none of her bones had been broken and bravely declared that she was determined to carry on. Someone said that the fall could be serious and suggested they phone for an ambulance so that she could be taken to hospital for a thorough examination. Wincing with pain, Jackie said they couldn't do that, in case it caused a breach in security.

Despite all Jackie's protestations the Old Order carried her upstairs and laid her on her bed to rest. She overheard them whispering that the whole operation could be jeopardised if, in her present state, she insisted on flying with them. She heard words being bandied about such as "encumbrance" and "a menace to the whole operation." They pleaded with her to stay at home in bed, to try and recover.

Reluctantly, Jackie agreed and her guests trooped off downstairs for more coffee and a last piece of cake.

When the bedroom door closed behind them, Jackie waited for the sound of their footsteps to fade away before reaching out for the telephone that lay on the bedside table. She dialled a number. A voice came over the line, "Betty Bright speaking."

"Hi, Betty, it's Jackie here." She then gave the chief of intelligence a full account of the council of war meeting. When she had finished speaking, Betty Bright said, "Thank you, Jackie."

"You can cut out the thanks," said Jackie, speaking harshly. "Just do what you always do. Bring the money to me personally. Cash, mind you. Tomorrow morning, early – that will be fine, okay?"

"Of course, dear Jackie. Tomorrow morning, early – yes, that will be fine. That's the deal, isn't it? Oh, but before I go, tell me, Jackie, how do you feel about betraying all those people who trusted you?"

Without hesitation, Jackie replied, "Richer," and without saying goodbye she returned the telephone to the bedside table.

After speaking to Jackie Fife, the chief of intelligence went to the commandant's office and knocked on the door. A fellow security officer was already in the room and so was a handsome young stranger. They were deep in conversation. The commandant broke off the talk when Betty entered the room.

"Hi, Betty," she said, "allow me to introduce you to Megan's brother from Cader Idris. He's here to help us."

"Thank you, Ma'am," said the chief of intelligence to the commandant, and then she shook hands with the sorcerer. "I know of your work," she said to him. "Thanks for agreeing to help us."

"Glad to," said the sorcerer.

"By the way," said Betty, "Thea and Phoebe will be in the first wave, leading the attack."

The sorcerer raised his eyebrows. "Thea and Phoebe, they're very skilful magicians. But not to worry, I can deal with them."

The commandant brought the meeting to order so that plans to defeat the attackers could be discussed. It was agreed that when all the explosives planted by Red One had been discovered, the charges would be removed but the detonators would be allowed to remain. The commandant explained the reason for that. "I want them to think that everything is going to plan," she said. "The security officer tells us that detonators will make a lot of noise but won't cause much damage. So, let us leave it like that. The noise will signal them to begin the attack and they'll come charging in. It's supposed to be a surprise attack, but, thanks to our chief of intelligence, forewarned is to be forearmed and we'll be ready for them."

The commandant then asked each of them in turn to make a contribution to the defence plans and so the meeting continued.

CHAPTER FOURTEEN

A BANQUET IN HONOUR OF UCHTRED

After they had demolished Jackie's food the Old Order of witches brought up chairs from downstairs and crowded into her bedroom to watch the latest TV news on the arrival of the spaceship from Petranova.

Before the spaceship touched down there was an interview with Professor Klopstock and his nephew, Eliot, who had both just flown in from San Francisco. Then the professor's friend, the American air force general, spoke and he talked glowingly of Anglo-American relationships. He waxed lyrically about the hands of friendship that the peoples of America and Great Britain were reaching out to those who lived on other planets. The media lapped it up, but there was no doubt as to who stole the show. It was Lindsey! In front of the camera she described a dream that she had had the previous night. In her dream she was flying in a spaceship with Jupiter and Alison and some boys and girls from her class at school – they were flying to the moon. When she looked down they could see the earth no larger than her brother Alex's coloured football with bits of mud sticking to it! The interviewer laughed and asked if, in her dream, she had been scared to be flying so high up and so far away from the planet earth. "Oh no," she replied, "It was lovely." As she spoke, her large brown eyes seemed to grow wider with wonder. The media world fell in love with her. They fell in love with Leanne, Alison and Laura too. Laura's American accent drew them to her like a magnet and when they discovered that it was her map that had led the Ponyteers to the Roman treasure cave on the Sandstone Trail in an earlier adventure, she was besieged by reporters and bombarded with questions. In the end she had to be rescued by Professor Klopstock and Eliot.

After their interviews Leanne whispered to her sister, "When you told Alison and me about your dream, Lindsey, you told us that it was just Alison, John Williams and Peter Snowdon who were with you. But, you didn't mention the boys' names to the interviewer. You said, boys and girls from your class were with you in the spaceship dream."

"I know I did," Lindsey whispered back. "But, if I'd mentioned John and Peter's names while we were on telly, what do you think it would have been like for Alison and me at school tomorrow? Go on, Leanne, tell us what you would have done?"

Leanne was not the sort of person who made a habit of telling fibs, but she agreed that given the same situation, she would have said the same as her sister.

The TV news bulletin had now focussed on the spaceship, which touched down exactly on time. Uchtred, leader of the "gentle people" was the first to appear and as he descended the steps of the spaceship he and his advisers were given a rousing cheer of welcome from the large crowd that had assembled to greet him.

Jupiter came out last and was immediately mobbed by the Ponyteers. "It was cool, man, real cool," were the very first words that he uttered when he planted his metallic feet back on planet earth.

The city council of Chester had laid on a banquet in honour of Uchtred. The mayor and Uchtred shook hands with all the banquet guests as they arrived. Then Uchtred, as leader of the Petranovians, sat at the head of the table with the mayor and his wife. Sitting alongside them was the professor, his nephew and the American general. Before grace, the mayor stood up and made a welcoming speech to Uchtred. The technical experts from Petranova had erected a giant screen on one of the walls of the dining chamber and it soon became evident why. They had also installed the thought transference equipment that made it possible for Uchtred to understand what the mayor was saying and for everybody to understand what he had to say in reply.

Somehow, a Japanese delegate's thoughts got onto the screen. "I'll give you a billion dollars, Uchtred, for the secret of your thought transference equipment."

"Not negotiable, don't even think about it," flashed up Uchtred's instant reply to the sound of tumultuous laughter.

After the dinner ended Uchtred stayed with the mayor and his wife as their special guest while the professor and his American friend, general Bill Ferguson, returned to Tinsall to stay at the Boot Inn.

Just after eleven o'clock that night, as they were strolling through the grounds of the inn discussing what a great success the dinner had been, Bill Ferguson confided that if commitments in the States allowed, he too, would accompany the professor to Petranova for what was surely going to be a most fantastic holiday.

Conversation petered out a little as jet lag took its toll on the two elderly men; all they wanted now was a good night's sleep. They were about to enter the door of the inn when Bill stopped in his tracks. He gripped the professor's arm so tightly the pressure made him wince. "Look up there, Jules," he said hoarsely, pointing up to the night sky.

Jules looked up and there, in the sky, almost over Chester and silhouetted against the moon, he counted what appeared to be three flights of witches.

"I must be cracking up, Jules," the general said in a weak voice. "And please don't tell anyone I said this, but just now I thought I saw a whole bunch of witches up there. I had a similar experience last time I was here, remember?"

The professor was sympathetic. He couldn't bear to see his friend so troubled and anxious. He said, "Yes, I remember what happened last time and, no, you're not cracking up, Bill. What you've seen tonight is real. I should have told you the full story before, but I didn't think you would believe me." He took his friend by the arm. "Come inside, its time you knew what's been going on here."

Once they were inside and settled down comfortably, the professor began his story. He started at the very beginning and he reminded Bill of the terrible explosion that had taken place when the original robot, Jupiter, had accidentally self-destructed at his house in San Francisco.

"I know about that," said Bill Ferguson, interrupting. "It cost the air force and the US government a lot of money." Recollection of what had happened made him shake his head. He muttered, "It sure did cost us a lot of money."

"Don't remind me," said the professor, waving his hand and the memory aside. And then he went on to tell his friend about the map he had given to Laura that enabled the Ponyteers to find the Roman treasure cave, only to be locked in it and left to die by the murderous couple, Mr and Mrs W E R Crookes. "It was Juno who rescued them," he said.

127

"Ah, Juno, that reminds me," said Bill. "Those robots, Jules. I know the president himself gave permission for Jupiter to make that original trip to Petranova, but when you return this time, we want you and the robots back in the States. We need you, okay?"

"What do you mean, you need me and the robots back in the States?"

"Well, things have been happening, Jules. The air force needs you. I've got plans and you, Juno and Jupiter are part of them. Look, we need to talk."

"Okay, okay, we will talk, but later. I thought you wanted to know about that bunch of witches you saw in the sky outside?"

"Oh, I do. I do. Go on, tell me the rest, we can talk about my plans later."

"Okay," said the professor, and then he went on to tell his friend about the witch's den, Mrs Eastly's den, that Alex and Ginger Tomkins had discovered on a visit to Red House Farm and the threats that had been made against them. "I think you know about the rest," said the professor. "You know about the battle that took place under the dark side of the hill, and the events that led to the president granting permission for Jupiter to fly Uchtred and the 'gentle people' back to Petranova."

"Yes, yes, Jules. I know about that," said Bill Ferguson, heaving a big sigh. "And thanks for filling me in about those witches and stuff. Guess I'll sleep like a log tonight, now I know that I'm not going crazy."

The relaxed look on Bill's face was enough to make the professor feel that he, too, would have a good night's sleep.

As he was unlocking the door to his room, Bill turned round to remark, "That formation those witches were flying, Jules. Looked like they were going to war."

128

"Perhaps they were, Bill. Perhaps they were." The professor was too tired to explain to his friend that rumours of conflict between the Old Order and the New Order could, at any moment, burst into an all-out war. He said instead, "Good night, Bill, sleep well." He waited until his friend closed the door behind him and then went into his own room. He undressed and climbed into bed. He thought about the war-like formation the witches were flying and as he closed his eyes, he wondered what would be the outcome of their conflict. He was still puzzling over that when he finally fell asleep.

CHAPTER FIFTEEN

THE ATTACK

Red One calculated that the tail wind would make them ten minutes early. To take care of this, she led the formation into a wide, time-wasting circuit behind a clump of trees. They were flying low – and the trees – which grew only a short distance from their target, also provided safe cover from HQ radar. Radio monitoring went on throughout the whole 24 hours of the day at HQ, so Ruth had insisted that radio silence be strictly observed – and it was. The airwaves were silent. Not a whisper could be heard.

Looking at the luminous dial of her watch, Red One saw that it was twelve o'clock, midnight! Three loud reports rang out! The explosions were strong enough to shake the trees and the witches rocked slightly on their broomsticks in the turbulence that followed the blasts. But the shock wave quickly disappeared and regaining control of their broomsticks, the witches flew on, convinced that victory was within their grasp.

Breaking radio silence, Red One spoke into her microphone. Her voice rang out loud and clear, "Attack! Attack! Attack!" she commanded. "Back door! Back door!"

The witches Thea and Phoebe obeyed instantly. They set their broomsticks into a shallow dive to increase speed and did a tight turn to take them to the rear of the building. The back door looked as if it had been blasted open by explosives, it sagged on its hinges. But it was all a ploy, the doors hinges had been purposely loosened and the sorcerer was waiting for them to enter.

Seeing the back door partially open, Thea and Phoebe released a powerful force of demons to spearhead their attack. The evil spirits appeared in all shapes and sizes, some changing colour as they flew. Then the howling began. Those inside the building trembled with fear when they saw and heard what was happening. They tried to hide – under tables, desks, anywhere – away from the devils that were shrieking and seeking to kill them. But the sorcerer did not hide. He suddenly appeared in the doorway, dressed in his splendid robe of scarlet and gold and carrying his magic wand in his right hand. Seeing him, the demons howled louder than ever, speeding towards him, intent on his destruction. But the sorcerer stood his ground. He opened his arms wide and cried out in a loud voice:

Evil spirits, I end your reign,
Perish in this magic flame.

Then he pointed his wand against the advancing horde and great thunderbolts and jagged flashes of lightening blasted into them, reducing the demons into tiny particles of harmless dust. A mighty tornado-like wind sprang up, sucking up the dust and hurling it into oblivion. Then, as quickly as its force had sprung up, the power of the wind died down. The silence of the still air was eerie. Thea and Phoebe, having witnessed magic far more powerful than their own, turned and fled in terror. The rest of the attacking force had seen enough, they scattered in all directions, desperate to escape.

CHAPTER SIXTEEN

THE BETRAYER IS PUNISHED

Fleeing from the scene of the battle, Mrs Eastly found Red One flying beside her. Bertha was frightened; the Old Order had been defeated and her attempt to overthrow her cousin had failed. In fact the whole operation had been a complete shambles, a disaster, there was no other way to describe it. She spoke nervously into her microphone, "Where shall we go, what shall we do now, Red One?"

Red One flew closer to her and shouted, "For a start, you can stop using that radio, Bertha. If you want to tell me something, or ask me something – shout! They'll be monitoring our frequency, okay?"

Mrs Eastly kept as close as she could to her companion and shouted, "Okay, Red One, I won't use the radio."

"That's okay then. Follow me back to Chester and stop calling me Red One. My days as Red One are over and you agreed to call me Ruth, remember?"

"Sorry, Red One, I mean Ruth. But why Chester? I would have thought that's the last place to visit. I mean, is it safe to go there?"

"There's no safe place for us now, Bertha, not in this country. But I've got a score to settle with that 'Jack The Knife'. She's the one who stabbed us in the back all right. She's nothing but a traitor and there she was, pretending to be your friend and a friend of the Old Order. Some friend! Jackie Fife, she's a traitor and a spy, Bertha. She's in the pay of the chief of security, Betty Bright, can't you see that?"

Mrs Eastly nearly fell off her broomstick in disbelief. "Surely Jackie wouldn't do a thing like that to her friends – to me?"

"Oh, wouldn't she? Work it out, Bertha. She waited until we had completed our plans, then she had that accident that landed her at the bottom of the stairs. It was all faked, Bertha. She didn't fall at all, we were the ones who did the falling and we fell for it, hook, line and sinker! I wager she was on the phone to betray us to Betty Bright the moment we left her bedroom. Well, now it's payback time." Ruth's jaw was set. Bertha had never seen her in this mood before, she looked positively fierce and threatening. She kept darting glances at her as they flew towards Chester, but the expression on Ruth's face didn't alter, it remained dark and grim and threatening.

It was around two o'clock in the morning when they arrived at Jackie Fife's house and a light was shining through her bedroom window. The curtains had not been drawn, so they hovered outside on their broomsticks, able to see everything that was happening inside. A large wooden chest stood in a corner of the room. They saw Jackie kneel down to open it. It took two keys to unlock it. The lid was heavy, but Jackie was strong, she lifted the lid and sent it crashing against the wall. For a few moments she stayed on her knees looking at the contents of the chest. She had a very strange look in her eyes.

"Just look at her," said Ruth, speaking into Mrs Eastly's ear. "Just look at her, down on her knees, you'd think she was worshiping what she's got in that box."

"Perhaps she is, Ruth. She loves money; everybody knows it. But I never thought it would come to this. I mean, you know, sell her friends for money."

They watched Jackie scoop up a bundle of notes from the chest and deposit them on the bed. She repeated her visit to the chest several times, each of her visits adding to the mounting pile of notes. Then the counting began. Every now and again she would pause, stop counting and caress her cheeks with some of the banknotes. Another time she would scoop as many bundles of notes from the bed as she could possibly carry in both hands, then, after pressing them lovingly to her lips she would allow them to flutter back onto the bed. Absorbed, they watched as the whole process began all over again. Throughout this procedure, Jackie's face remained taut and pale and her eyes seemed to bulge as she stared fixedly at the money.

They had seen enough. Ruth signalled to Mrs Eastly and the witches glided silently down to ground level where Ruth indicated to Bertha that she should accompany her to the front door. Once there, Ruth gave a loud knock. They heard Jackie's voice calling out. She was expecting someone – that much was clear. Ruth placed her finger to her lips and whispered for Bertha to stay quiet. Jackie spoke clearly as she was opening the door, "That was quick, Betty. Don't tell me it's over already? Hope you've brought the cash with…" She stopped in mid sentence and almost collapsed. The two people standing in front of her were the last two people in the world she had expected to see.

Ruth and Bertha pushed Mrs Fife inside and led her into the lounge. They forced her to sit down in a chair

135

and Ruth nodded towards Mrs Eastly, who was standing behind her.

Jackie was stuttering and stammering, but words failed her.

Bertha sprinkled some magic powder over Jackie's head, chanting the incantation:

> *With this magic powder and sign of the snake*
> *Into a mangy old parrot I thee make.*

Instantly, Mrs Fife disappeared and in the chair where she had been sitting was a mangy old parrot.

Mrs Eastly was ecstatic. "See that, Ruth," she cried. "I can get it right, sometimes."

"Good for you, Bertha," said Ruth, congratulating her.

The parrot on the chair flapped its wings and squawked, "I'm Jackie Fife. I'm Jackie Fife. I'll have you know that I'm a very rich lady. I'm a very rich lady. I'm a very rich lady…"

"Shurrup! You're talking like a parrot," said Ruth abruptly, and Bertha shook with laughter.

When Bertha had stopped laughing Ruth asked her to collect some warm bedding.

"Why, where are we staying?"

"Well, it won't be the Grosvenor, that's for sure," confided Ruth. "Look, Bertha, it's cold outside, so collect as much as you can carry. Oh, and bring a few candles too, that's if you find any."

Bertha shivered. Already she was feeling cold and when she thought of the future, she shuddered; the future looked as cold as the iciest winter.

She searched around and found a few candles in a kitchen cupboard. She put them in her pocket and then set about collecting the bedding. When she had put together as much as she could carry, she reported to Ruth who warned her they must leave quickly. "No time to waste," she said. "If I were Betty Bright, this would be one of the first places I'd investigate."

As they opened the door, the parrot began squawking again, "I'm Jackie Fife. I'm Jackie Fife. I'm a rich lady. I'm a very rich lady…"

"Take no heed of her, Bertha. Her days of betrayal are over. No one will listen to a word of what she has to say now." Ruth's voice was charged with smug satisfaction. And why not? She had accomplished what she had set out to do.

Bertha closed the door behind them. They mounted their broomsticks and flew away from the house. Within seconds the sound of the parrot's squawks had completely faded away.

About two hours later, Betty Bright arrived at Jackie Fife's house. She called out to Jackie from the hall, "The door wasn't locked, Jackie, so I came right in." She looked around. "Where are you, Jackie?"

"I'm here," squawked the parrot from the lounge.

Betty entered the room and the sight she saw almost made her turn and run away. A mangy old parrot was strutting up and down on the back of a chair. When it saw Betty, the parrot began to squawk, "The money. Have you brought the money? The money. Have you brought the money?" It kept repeating the same question.

"Yes, I've brought the money," Betty's reply came out in a whisper.

"Then put it on the table. I said, put it on the table. Put it on the table." On and on squawked the parrot, repeating every phrase in a monotonous squawk.

Betty's hands were trembling as she put the money on the table. Speechless, she turned to leave the room. The parrot croaked after her, "I'm Jackie Fife, I'm a rich lady, I'm a very rich lady. I'm Jackie Fife, I'm a very rich lady…"

As she stood in the sanctuary of the doorway, Betty recovered sufficiently to reply, "No, Jackie, not any more, you're not. That's who and what you used to be. I'll tell you what you are now, shall I? You're just a pathetic, greedy, mangy old parrot that squawked once too often. You betrayed your friends, they found you out and now you're paying the price!"

Betty's dealings with Jackie were ended for good. She never did like her, not even a bit. Well, how could she like any of her spies who accepted money for betraying their friends? It was just a nasty side of her job and she had to put up with it. She closed the door and strode briskly down the street with her broomstick tucked under her arm. The squawking from the parrot followed her for a while, but in the time it took her to walk less than a dozen paces the awful croaking sound had died away.

Betty could always think more clearly when she was walking, so she walked. What had happened to "Jack The Knife" was totally unexpected and what Betty now needed was someone who could fill the spot she had vacated. Her mind slipped into overdrive. Within seconds she had come up with the answer, she knew exactly who that person should be. With her mind made up and despite the early hour, she set course to see Thea, the witch who lived on the border between Chester and North Wales.

"Smart girl," mused Betty to herself. She was now sitting comfortably on her broomstick and was well on her way to Thea's. But it wasn't Thea she was thinking about; it was Red One. She guessed, quite rightly, that Red

138

One had worked out who had done the betraying and that it must have been she and Bertha Eastly who had taken their revenge on Jackie. Betty couldn't help smiling. The decision to change "Jack The Knife" into a parrot, somehow it seemed so – appropriate.

Betty alighted outside Thea's house and banged on the door with her broomstick handle. She could hear Thea's grumbling voice as she came up the passage. Thea opened the door, quickly trying to close it again when she saw who was standing outside. Betty was too agile for her, jamming the door open with her foot. Thea fled up the passage, planning to escape by the back door. Betty called after her sharply, "No, no, Thea. We haven't come to arrest you. I'm on my own. Listen to me, Thea, I've come to do a deal with you."

Thea stopped in her tracks and returned to the front door. Looking furtively up and down the street to make sure it was clear of people, she said, "You'd better come inside, we can talk in the parlour."

The chief of intelligence explained that Jackie's cover had been blown and that she would have to be replaced. She came to the point quickly. "This is the deal, Thea. Work for me undercover and you'll be protected. Refuse – and you will spend the rest of your days on Black Rock. What do you say?"

Thea didn't hesitate. "I'll work for you," she said.

"Good," said Betty. "We'll talk some more later. All I want to do right now is go to bed. I feel I could sleep for a week!" She looked at her watch. It was past five o'clock in the morning.

Ruth had flown with Mrs Eastly from Jackie Fife's house and now they were standing outside the old Roman treasure cave on the Sandstone Trail.

"So this is where we're going to spend the night, is it?" said Mrs Eastly, disdainfully.

Ruth ignored the remark, "We'll be safe here, at least for tonight," she said. Then, thrusting her hand into a hole in the rock she located the ratchet wheel that, when turned, would open the entrance to the cave. But, the ratchet wheel would not turn – it was locked! The curators had put a lock and chain on it when they were taking away the treasure and artefacts to the museum in Chester. Undeterred, Ruth muttered a few words from a secret spell and the chain snapped. The lock flew open and she was able to turn the ratchet wheel until a gap appeared in the wall of the cave. When it was wide enough she crawled through and peered down. But the cave was dark and she couldn't see the floor, so Ruth crossed her fingers, shut her eyes and jumped. Luckily, it was barely two metres to the floor and, agile as a cat, Ruth landed safely on her feet.

Mrs Eastly could not follow her, because somehow she had managed to get her bottom wedged in the entrance gap. Hanging down, head first, she felt trapped and frightened. Flailing her arms about wildly she was unable to struggle free. She gasped, "You'll have to help me, Ruth."

Ruth jumped up and caught hold of Mrs Eastly's belt. Bracing her feet on the wall of the cave she gave one mighty heave and Mrs Eastly shot out of the gap like a cork from a champagne bottle. They fell in a heap on the floor of the cave, Mrs Eastly landing on top! Ruth rolled Mrs Eastly away from her and gasped, "How that old broomstick of yours puts up with you, Bertha, I'll never know," and she laughed.

Mrs Eastly struggled to get up from the floor. She didn't very much like Ruth's last remark and if there had been any light in the cave it would have illuminated the scowl of disapproval that distorted her features.

The cave was not quite as cold as they had expected, nevertheless they were glad of the warm bedding they had brought with them from Jackie Fife's house. Mrs Eastly produced the candles she had found in Jackie's kitchen. She lit them and they could see that the cave was bare. But the light from the candles was comforting and in their glow, the cave seemed just a little bit cosier.

Eventually, they settled down for the night. In a few seconds Mrs Eastly could hear the sound of Ruth's deep breathing, already she was fast asleep.

Although desperately tired, Mrs Eastly could not sleep. Resentment kept her awake. She had failed at everything she had set out to do and that made her very angry. She had failed in her efforts to hurt the so-called Ponyteers and she had failed to defeat her cousin Mabel. And once again she was on the run – a fugitive – and this time there was no place left in the whole world in which she could safely hide. Under her blankets she crossed her fingers, hoping that perhaps Ruth would find a solution.

She left the candles to burn down and it was almost dawn before Mrs Eastly finally fell asleep.

CHAPTER SEVENTEEN

WHO'S GOING TO PETRANOVA?

Ruth slept well. It was eight o'clock in the morning and after just a few hours' sleep she felt as fresh as a daisy. She started to shake Mrs Eastly and continued to shake her until she opened her sticky eyes. Mrs Eastly wasn't ready to be awakened and showed her disapproval by pushing Ruth away. She said irritably, "Don't, Ruth, don't do that. Can't you see I'm tired?"

Ruth stopped shaking her and said, sympathetically, "Sorry, Bertha, I know you're tired. And you've had such a rotten time over the past few weeks – really bad – I know, I know, and I'm sorry." She knelt beside Mrs Eastly and patted her head. "Poor dear, ever since your cousin, Mabel, confined you to Black Rock it's been downhill all the way, hasn't it? In prison and all that stress, you must have had a dreadful time. And on the night of your escape, just as things seemed to be going nicely, we had that terrible crash over Tinsall. Horrible! We were lucky to get away with that, Bertha – we could have been killed, you know. And after, when I had been rescued and was tucked up nice and cosy in my bed, I thought of you, Bertha, I thought how frightening it must have been for you having to walk in the dark, all the way to Jackie Fife's house in Chester."

Mrs Eastly said, "Frightened? I'll say. Half the time I didn't know where I was. It was sheer luck that led me to Jackie's house."

"Well, and we all know what happened there, don't we?" said Ruth. "Jackie Fife – traitor that she is – betrayed us. We lost the battle at HQ and all because of Jackie Fife, we're on the run." She looked at Mrs Eastly, whose eyelids were drooping, "Of course you are tired, Bertha. We are all tired, we've hardly had any sleep for three days."

Mollified by some of the things that Ruth had said, Mrs Eastly stopped complaining – but not for long!

Less than two minutes later, she stretched out her heavy body under the blankets, and said, "Ooh, did you hear that?"

"Hear what?" asked Ruth.

Mrs Eastly stretched again. "There," she said, "Did you hear it that time? Did you hear my bones cracking?"

"Didn't hear a thing," said Ruth.

Mrs Eastly snorted, "Well, listen when I tell you. My poor old bones can't take much more of this. It's cold, Ruth, and I'm frozen."

Mrs Eastly was the complainer of complainers, Ruth knew that, and she tried to cheer Mrs Eastly up in the best way she knew how – by pretending to be a complainer herself. Striking an angry pose, she said in a loud voice, "You're quite right, Bertha, it is cold. And those Romans, I think it's awful, I really do. Now wouldn't you think that if they were the clever clogs they're supposed to have been, they would have installed some of their warm central heating into this cave when they made it? Just why they didn't is quite beyond me." Ruth waited for Mrs Eastly to laugh, but she

143

was silent and Ruth realized that her attempt at humour had fallen as flat as the cave floor she was standing on.

From one of the zipped pockets in her flying suit Mrs Eastly had discovered some paper and a pen and was writing something down when the candles suddenly flickered. Startled, Bertha looked up from her writing. "Ooh! What's happening?" she cried out.

Ruth reassured her, "It's just a flicker. Don't worry, those candles will be burning long after we've gone from this place." She looked at Bertha, whose forehead was creased in concentration whilst she applied pen to paper, and was curious. "Don't tell me you're writing your last will and testament, Bertha?"

"No, most certainly I'm not," said Mrs Eastly, emphatically. She finished her writing, put away her pen and began to explain what it was that had kept her so busy. "I've been writing to my solicitors…"

She was interrupted by Ruth. "I thought you said you weren't writing your last will and testament, Bertha?"

Mrs Eastly answered irritably, "I've already told you that I'm not writing my last will and testament. How many more times do I have to tell you? If you'll just listen, instead of interrupting all the time, then you'll find out why, won't you?"

"Sorry," said Ruth, as meekly as she could.

"Right. Well, I've been writing to inform them that I shall be out of the country for quite some time and don't really know when I'll be back."

She paused to make sure that Ruth had taken in what she had said. Then she added triumphantly, "And I've instructed them to let the twins have Red House Farm." Again there was a pause while she scanned Ruth's face, looking for a response.

"I think the letter's a brilliant idea," said Ruth. "And that bit about leaving the country and not knowing when you'd be back – nice touch that, Bertha. It should put Mabel off for a while. As for leaving Red House Farm to the twins, I like that bit best of all. Helps to put right all those…" Ruth stopped, she seemed to be stuck for words – she faltered and then started the sentence again, "It helps to put right some of those past misunderstandings, doesn't it?"

Mrs Eastly sneered. "Past misunderstandings? What are you talking about? I didn't hand the farm over to them to make amends. I did it for me. Did it for us. When Mabel gets to hear about it, she'll think that I've gone away for good. It'll put her off the scent and give us more time. As for the twins, I've no love for them. In fact, I hate them. I've always hated them. But I hate them even more for deserting me like they did. To tell you honestly, Ruth, if they were here right now I'd give 'em something to think about. Put some spells on them. You bet I would." The old cruel look was back in her eyes again. In truth, it was never really far away.

She stood up and stretched, the blankets falling in a heap on the sandy floor. "Ooh! We can't stay in this place forever, Ruth, my poor old bones can't take it."

"Well, we don't have to stay here forever," said Ruth, brightly. "Just say the word, Bertha, and we'll be out of here, today – and forever!"

"How do you mean, out of here today and forever?" said Mrs Eastly.

"Means exactly what it says. And it all depends on you, Bertha. It all depends on whether you fancy a nice long holiday, or not."

"Holiday! Are you losing your senses, Ruth? How can we possibly go on holiday with my cousin, Mabel, and all that lot breathing down our necks? They'd root us out wherever we went."

"Not where I've got in mind," grinned Ruth.

Bertha stopped to think, but gave up to ask, "Oh, and where the heck is that?"

"Petranova," came Ruth's calm reply.

"Petranova! You're pulling my leg. It's a joke. You're having me on, Ruth, right?"

"No, no, I'm deadly serious, Bertha. You said that no matter where we went, your cousin would root us out and I'm convinced you are right about that. But Petranova; your cousin's tentacles couldn't possibly stretch that far, now could they?"

Mrs Eastly was beginning to show some interest, so Ruth continued, "We'd be safe there, Bertha. Just think, you could have a nice long rest." She laughed, "And if you get bored, you could always start up a 'Sisterhood' in Petranova."

That really amused Bertha, and now she started to laugh, laughing so much the flesh on her body rippled over her bones like jelly on a plate.

"Okay, Ruth," she said when she was composed again. "You're on. I'll go to Petranova with you." But then she became suspicious of Ruth's intentions, "Look here, Ruth, if this is a joke…"

"I've told you, it's not a joke," said Ruth seriously. "Honestly, Bertha, it isn't."

"But how do we get on the spaceship without being spotted?"

Ruth explained how they could do it.

"But would it work? Honestly, Ruth, I don't have the magic," said Mrs Eastly, speaking truthfully for once.

"But I have," said Ruth confidently. "And it would work

too, if only we had some magic dust. Snag is, I haven't brought any with me."

A look of triumph crossed Mrs Eastly's face. Plunging her hand into another zipped pocket of her flying suit she brought out a small box which she held aloft. "Full," she cried. "This box is full of magic dust."

"That's it then," said Ruth. "Our holiday in Petranova is definitely on."

Ruth expected to see Mrs Eastly smile, but found instead that she was looking distinctly miserable. "What's the matter, Bertha, I thought you'd be happy?"

"Oh, I am," said Mrs Eastly, "I am happy, but I'm hungry, Ruth. The last bite to cross my lips was the buffet at Jackie Fife's. I'm starving, Ruth. Really starving."

Ruth seemed to have a solution for everything. "Tell you what, Bertha," she said, "You de-programme those broomsticks and bury them here in the cave with our flying gear. And while you're doing that I'll pop up to the corner shop and get us something to eat, okay?"

"Okay," said Bertha. And she handed Ruth the letter she had been writing to her solicitors. "Buy an envelope and a stamp while you are there and post it for me, will you, Ruth? Their address is on the letter. Do you need any money?"

"No, that's all right, I've plenty of change. But where we're going, maybe they don't use money there. Wow! Think about it. I'll be off then, Bertha, back in less than half an hour. Don't forget, bury those broomsticks, okay?"

Mrs Eastly watched Ruth leap up and fasten her hands on the ledge that surrounded the opening to the cave. She hauled herself up like an acrobat, wriggled through the narrow aperture and disappeared into the world outside.

Mrs Eastly began to work on the sandy floor of the cave, making it ready to bury their broomsticks and flying gear. But she was a very lazy person by nature and soon tired of digging and scraping holes with her shoes in the sand. As for de-programming the broomsticks, she could not be bothered with that. In the end she just bundled the lot into a narrow trench, piled sand over them and smoothed it down. Easy. She stood back to admire her work.

Pretending to be busy, she began to flick sand about the floor when she heard Ruth climbing in through the opening to the cave.

"Eat first, talk later," said Ruth, handing sandwiches and milk to Mrs Eastly.

Bertha didn't argue with her. She tucked into her sandwiches and drank her milk without speaking a word. When she had finished, she licked her lips and burped with satisfaction.

Ruth looked at her watch. It was eleven thirty. "Come on, Madam," she said, briskly. "It's holiday time and your carriage awaits you."

Bertha looked up at the opening of the cave above them and her heart sank. "I can't get up there." She had an anxious look on her face. "You won't leave me here, will you, Ruth?"

"Don't be daft," said Ruth, " Friends don't do things like that. And don't worry, Bertha, we'll have you out of here in next to no time." She pointed to the coil of rope she had wound round her waist. "When I throw the rope down to you, Bertha, all you have to do is to tie it securely round your middle and hold on tight. Leave the rest to me, okay?"

"Okay," Bertha said weakly, and she watched with envy as Ruth made her agile exit from the cave. As she waited for the rope to come tumbling down to her, Bertha, who had never had a friend in her life, wondered just how long it would be before Ruth got tired of doing things for her and abandoned her…

In the village of Tinsall events unfolded which had never been witnessed there before. Mr Gribe, the local reporter, or "Gribe The Scribe" as the locals more affectionately knew him, was very happy. The lords of the media who wanted to know all he could tell them about the Ponyteers and their past adventures besieged him, thirsty for news. They were in good hands, Gribe did not let them down; he had reported every one of the girls' adventures in the local newspaper. Word for word, he remembered them, so he took his time and slowly and with great relish he repeated every one of them. Reporters from national newspapers listened to him making copious notes and for a little while "Gribe The Scribe" became the most important journalist in the country!

The interviews were taking place at the Boot Inn, in the village. The inn had been specially decked out with flags for the occasion, there was a holiday mood in the air and happy chattering people occupied all the outside tables and chairs, waiting for the spaceship to take off for Petranova. The longer they waited, the greater their excitement became. Glinting in the warm sun, as it sat in the centre of the field adjacent to the inn, the spaceship seemed to be sending out signals to the people who were watching, "Don't give up," the signals seemed to be saying, "Be patient. Keep watching and soon, at take-off, you'll see just how powerful I really am!"

Professor Klopstock and the American general sat at one of the inn's tables and the professor's nephew,

Eliot, brought up some more tables and chairs so that the Ponyteers and their parents could join them. "Where's Alex?" the professor asked Laura.

"Gone for a walk with Ginger Tomkins. They'll be part way up the Sandstone Trail, but he'll be back for the take-off," she said.

"Hope so," said the professor. "It'll be a sight he'll remember for the rest of his life."

He patted Laura affectionately on the head, then went back to talk to his nephew and the general.

Laura's grandparents were chatting to Leanne and Lindsey's parents. "We've got a parrot," Laura's granddad announced.

"A what?"

"It's true. It's a parrot. Just turned up at the door this morning." He laughed, "Sounds crazy, I know, but she kept saying she was Jackie Fife and a rich lady and that she was frightened of Red One. That's all we could get out of her. Luckily we had a cage from our last budgie. We opened the door and in she hopped. When we closed the door she calmed down a bit." Laura's Granddad spoke to Leanne's dad. "Come to think of it, Chris, she did say something else. She said she wanted to be kept locked in that cage and stay with us forever! Now, what do you make of that?"

"Incredible. Absolutely amazing. In this life you never know what's going to happen next, do you?" said Leanne's dad. All the company agreed.

"And who would believe such a story?" asked Laura's granddad. "But we have the parrot there at home, to prove that it's all true."

Alison and Lindsey were very quiet. Lindsey leaned over and whispered to Alison, "Can you see them?"

150

"Over there," whispered Alison, with a quick turn of her head.

Lindsey looked and saw the boys, John Williams and Peter Snowden. She gave them a smile and they smiled back. "I'm looking forward to that disco when we get home again. Both of them, they're great dancers," she said to Alison.

"And footballers," added Alison.

"Footballers! What's that got to do with it?" Lindsey said sharply.

"Nothing. I'm just saying, that's all."

"Huh! You sound like Alex. That's why he likes them, 'cos he says they're good footballers."

"Well, they are," said Alison. "And by the way, where's that brother of yours and his pal? They should be back by now."

"Don't worry, they'll be back. Back at the last minute, you'll see. You know how it is with Alex."

Alex and Ginger were on their way home to wave the Ponyteers goodbye on the trip to Petranova when, suddenly, Ginger stopped in his tracks. "Look! Alex. The treasure cave, the entrance – it's open! See the broken chain and lock. Somebody's been inside."

Alex picked up the length of rope that had been left behind by Ruth Davenport. "And this is what they must have used to help them climb in and out. Come on, Ginger, let's take a look inside and see what they've been up to."

Using the rope to help them, it took only a matter of minutes before they had landed inside the cave. A few candles were still burning and in the flickering light they saw the freshly disturbed sand on the floor. Within seconds they had unearthed the broomsticks and flying gear. They decided to leave the flying clothing in the cave but took the broomsticks and microphones with them, passing them to each other as they climbed out onto the hillside. They found a foxhole big enough to take all they had to hide and there they left it, to be collected and used later. That done, they ran as fast as they could down the hill so they would not be late for the spaceship's departure.

Meanwhile, Betty Bright took a taxi from headquarters to the Boot Inn, where she sat alone with an ice-cold drink of Coke to quench her thirst. Betty was very tired. She thought she had never felt so tired. She was seeing spots before her eyes. Her eyes were sore and she had difficulty in keeping them open. But today was important. Today was special; she forced herself to stay awake to witness the take-off to Petranova, and looked on wearily as the children said goodbye to their parents and friends.

At last the spaceship door was opened. Professor Klopstock and his nephew walked up the ramp together with the Ponyteers. The professor's false leg squeaked. As they reached the open door, the children stopped to call goodbye to the crowd.

In return John and Peter gave Lindsey and Alison a special farewell cheer. Then Leanne noticed Bill and Andy waving to her. She blushed as she acknowledged them.

"I think she likes me. I really think she likes me," they said in unison. Realizing what they had said, the twins laughed together as they turned again quickly to give Leanne a last wave.

The professor saluted his friend, the general, who drew himself to attention and returned the compliment.

Now the holidaymakers were all gathered together, crowding the entrance door to the spaceship. First, there was Uchtred, his advisors and crew, next to them Jupiter and Juno, then the professor and the Ponyteers.

A huge crowd had gathered to see them off and the newspaper photographers and television crews were filming away, while "Gribe The Scribe" was writing furiously in his notebook. In all the excitement, nobody except Betty Bright noticed the two little mice that ran up the ramp. She observed that one of them was sleek and lean and the other one rather fat and shaky on its legs. Each wore a necklace of sorts, with a tiny black bag attached to it. As they disappeared into the spaceship a thought crossed Betty's mind: could those mice be humans? But she shook her head, "Get a grip, Betty," she muttered to herself, "what you are thinking is crazy." She rubbed her eyes. They ached, and now she was seeing spots again. She could not decide what she had seen, or what to believe. Was it all just her imagination?

Finally, the door to the spaceship closed. There was a muffled roar from its power source, the crowd cheered and within seconds the spaceship had soared upwards and disappeared from sight.

"Gribe The Scribe" closed his notebook, the crowd dispersed and the media returned to their offices and studios. Only the families and friends of the Ponyteers were left behind, bidding tearful goodbyes to one another. Alex turned to Ginger, "Aren't grown-ups soppy?" he said. "Come on, let's get those broomsticks, we can hide them in the tree house now that Leanne and Lindsey have gone." Ginger nodded, and they were off like a shot to do just that.

On the Sandstone Trail a couple of hikers suddenly came to a halt as one of them stopped walking to listen intently to what he thought was loud cheering coming up from the village.

"Must be something special going on down there, don't you think?" he asked his friend.

"No way! I've told you before, nothing ever happens in Tinsall, absolutely nothing. It's that kind of village. So come on, we've a long way to go before it gets dark."

"Okay, okay, keep your shirt on, I'm coming."

The two hikers walked on. The village of Tinsall – the place where nothing ever happens – receded behind them until it became just a black speck in the distance. They turned around to have one last look, but Tinsall had disappeared – vanished! It was as though the village had never existed.